Praise for

The Marvelous Magic of Miss Mabel

"Wild fantasy, sly satire, and sharply observed family dynamics are the hallmarks of this tasty, effervescent series (along with mouthwatering recipes); this volume's the most delectable yet." —*Kirkus Reviews*

"Mabel's high jinks will appeal to readers of Roald Dahl's *Matilda* and Diana Wynne Jones's *Howl's Moving Castle*. . . . Mabel will inspire readers with her confident creativity." —*School Library Journal*

"This lovely celebration of quirky individualism applauds both creativity and science." —*Booklist*

"A tale full of rich imagery, it embraces the idea that family is not always where you come from, but who you are with. A fantasy story with a strong message of family, and believing in yourself." —*School Library Connection*

Also by Natasha Lowe

The Power of Poppy Pendle
The Courage of Cat Campbell

A Poppy Pendle novel

The Marvelous Magic of Miss Mabel

By Natasha Lowe

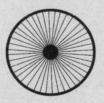

A PAULA WISEMAN BOOK

Simon & Schuster Books for Young Readers

New York   London   Toronto   Sydney   New Delhi

SIMON & SCHUSTER BOOKS FOR YOUNG READERS
An imprint of Simon & Schuster Children's Publishing Division
1230 Avenue of the Americas, New York, New York 10020
This book is a work of fiction. Any references to historical events,
real people, or real places are used fictitiously. Other names, characters, places,
and events are products of the author's imagination, and any resemblance to
actual events or places or persons, living or dead, is entirely coincidental.
Text copyright © 2016 by Natasha Lowe
Cover illustrations copyright © 2016 by Seb Mesnard
SIMON & SCHUSTER BOOKS FOR YOUNG READERS
is a trademark of Simon & Schuster, Inc.
For information about special discounts for bulk purchases, please contact Simon &
Schuster Special Sales at 1-866-506-1949 or business@simonandschuster.com.
The Simon & Schuster Speakers Bureau can bring authors to your live event. For more
information or to book an event, contact the Simon & Schuster Speakers Bureau
at 1-866-248-3049 or visit our website at www.simonspeakers.com.
Also available in a Simon & Schuster Books for Young Readers hardcover edition
Book design by Chloë Foglia
The text for this book was set in Cochin.
Manufactured in the United States of America
0820 OFF
First Simon & Schuster Books for Young Readers paperback edition August 2017
4 6 8 10 9 7 5 3
The Library of Congress has cataloged the hardcover edition as follows:
Names: Lowe, Natasha, author.
Title: The marvelous magic of Miss Mabel / Natasha Lowe.
Description: First edition. | New York : Simon & Schuster Books for Young Readers,
[2016] | "A Paula Wiseman Book." | Companion book to:
The courage of Cat Campbell, and The power of Poppy Pendle. |
Summary: "When young Mabel Ratcliff goes to study magic at Ruthersfield Academy,
she discovers not only that being a proper witch is harder than she thought, but also that
she is adopted"—Provided by publisher.
Identifiers: LCCN 2015048393 | ISBN 9781481465335 (hardback) |
ISBN 9781481465342 (paperback) | ISBN 9781481465359 (eBook)
Subjects: | CYAC: Witches—Fiction. | Magic—Fiction. | Self-realization—Fiction. |
Schools—Fiction. | Adoption—Fiction. | Foundlings—Fiction. | BISAC: JUVENILE
FICTION / Fantasy & Magic. | JUVENILE FICTION / Family / General (see also
headings under Social Issues). | JUVENILE FICTION / Social Issues / Friendship.
Classification: LCC PZ7.L9627 Mar 2016 | DDC [Fic]—dc23
LC record available at https://lccn.loc.gov/2015048393

In memory of my grandmothers, who dared to push boundaries and fly against the wind!

Betty Darling 1896–1982

Irene Ratcliff 1908–1998

✦ ✦ ✦

The Marvelous Magic of Miss Mabel

....

Chapter One

An Unusual Beginning

Saturday, April 23, 1887, 10:01 p.m.

THE NIGHT MABEL ARRIVED, NORA RATCLIFF WAS GETTING ready for bed. She had just taken the pins out of her hair and given it a good brush when a soft knocking sounded on the door. "Now, who in the world can that be?" Nora said, tying her nightcap under her chin as she hurried down the stairs. The Ratcliff residence was a sturdy brick house, three stories high, with a profusion of roses blooming in the garden, and when Nora opened the door, their fragrant scent wafted toward her on the warm, salty air. "Hello?" she called out, standing barefoot in her long white nightgown and straining her eyes against the gloom. There was nobody in sight. "Hello," she called again.

A snuffling noise came from one of the large terra-cotta flowerpots that stood on either side of the front door, and hurrying over, Nora Ratcliff found herself looking down into the scrunched-up face of a tiny baby.

A blanket of ferns covered the child, and she was nestled in the rich, soft earth, which Nora had been planning to plant lavender in. The baby squished handfuls of soil between her fingers and gazed solemnly up at Nora. She gave a tiny sneeze as an earthworm crawled over her foot. "And where in heavens did you come from?" Nora said, scooping the child into her arms. She hurried down the path and looked back and forth along Oak Lane.

On the other side of the road, huddled under a streetlamp, stood a young woman. Her hair was long and matted. She wore a ragged dress, and Nora could see that her feet were bare. Lifting her head, she looked over at Nora Ratcliff and with a great deal of anguish, choked out, "Please take care of my baby," just as a carriage came swaying around the corner.

The woman ran off, and Nora stepped back from the curb, cradling the infant close as the Cranfords' buggy trotted past. Returning from a late dinner somewhere, no doubt. Mrs. Cranford enjoyed her gossip as much as her food, and the sight of Nora Ratcliff standing outside in her nightgown, clutching a baby to her chest, would certainly set tongues wagging.

"I can't keep you, little one," Nora said wistfully. Nora's husband, Dr. Ratcliff, had been dead for ten years now, struck down by the influenza. Her parents were long buried, and she had not been blessed with children of her own. The baby reached out and grasped one of the ribbons on Nora's nightcap. She opened her eyes wide, and for a few moments they observed each other. From somewhere deep inside Nora, a vast well of feelings bubbled up, feelings from all the years of trying, and all the babies she couldn't have. It was at that precise instant that Nora Ratcliff suddenly and completely changed her mind.

"I shall call you Mabel," she announced to the night, "after my own mother." And hurrying back up the path, she was met at the door by her two housemaids, Daisy and Flora.

"I thought I heard noises," Daisy gasped. "Mam, what are you doing out here?"

"And *what* in heaven's name is that?" Flora said, her eyes fixed on the bundle in Nora's arms.

"It is a baby," Nora replied, swooping past them into the library. She nodded at the leather armchair, pulled up in front of the still smoldering fire. Daisy quickly removed a pile of books from the seat, and Nora settled herself into the chair. "This is Mabel," she said. "I found her in one of the flowerpots outside, and she will be living with me from now on."

Daisy opened her mouth, but no words came out.

Flora's face turned an angry crimson. "In a flowerpot," she squawked.

"Of course this will mean more work for you both, but I shall find a good nanny."

"No, mam. I mean yes, mam," Daisy said, grasping the back of the chair.

"This is an unusual situation, I am aware of that," Nora remarked, wondering at the sanity of her decision. "And if either of you feel the need to leave, I quite understand and will provide you with an excellent reference."

"Then I will be packing my bags and going," Flora said, her whole body wobbling with indignation. "You have no idea where that child is from. Living under the same roof as a flowerpot baby. I don't think so." And turning around, Flora marched from the room.

"Will you be needing a reference too, Daisy?" Nora asked with a sigh.

"Oh no, mam." Daisy gave her head a vigorous shake. "I would never do that, mam. You have always been good to me. And you don't need to go hiring any nursemaids," she added firmly. "I've got a soft spot for babies."

As word of Mabel's arrival spread, tongues most certainly did wag. Nora Ratcliff's baby was the talk of Melton Bay.

"Are you sure you know what you are getting in to?" Mrs. Cranford said the following afternoon. There had been a steady stream of ladies visiting the Ratcliff residence, drinking tea and nibbling currant cake while warning Nora of the horrors that awaited her.

"This is most unusual," Mrs. Fitzwilliam murmured.

"It is one thing to knit caps for the street urchins but quite another to bring one into your home," Mrs. Cranford advised. "You don't know where the child is from. You know nothing about her. Except that you found her in a flowerpot!"

"I know she needs a home," Nora replied boldly. But the ladies shook their heads in quiet disapproval, whispering behind their fans. And when it became clear that baby Mabel was there to stay, Nora found that the ladies of Melton Bay didn't visit quite so frequently. And in time she had no afternoon callers at all.

Mabel grew steadily, feeding on the boiled milk and sugar water that Daisy mixed together. Her hair sprouted like thistledown, and she liked to crawl around the house, trying to catch the sunbeams that danced across the rug. Every day she discovered something new, sticking her fingers into spiderwebs, or peeling apart a cabbage to find out what was inside. "Inquisitive little monkey, aren't you?" Daisy would say affectionately, removing Mabel from whatever mischief she had gotten in.

Nora believed it was all the good sea air that kept her daughter (for that is how she had come to think of Mabel) so healthy. As Mabel got older, she was often taken down to the beach. She liked to pick the hermit crabs up in her fingers and peer inside their shells. Mabel let them crawl over her legs, and one time popped a crab into her mouth to see if it tasted of the ocean. Little Eliza Cranford and her sisters would squeal in horror at such behavior, refusing to let Mabel join in their games. The nannies of Melton Bay had been instructed to keep their charges away from Mabel, and it was this, more than anything, that broke Nora's heart. Whenever Mabel trotted over to a group of children, wanting to show them her beach finds, they were ushered off to play somewhere else.

One hot August bank holiday, when Mabel was three, Nora took her to the pier to watch the Punch and Judy show. Mabel loved the little outdoor puppet theater, and they could hear children laughing as they made their way through the crowds. Hordes of day-trippers had taken the steam train into Melton Bay, and Nora held tight to Mabel's hand as they walked. She stopped for a moment in front of a stall selling baskets, letting go of Mabel briefly to examine a wide, flat basket, perfect for carrying roses.

"That's three shillings," the woman behind the counter said.

"It's lovely," Nora replied, admiring the tightness of the weave. She glanced down to check on Mabel, but there was no sign of her. Nora spun around wildly, her mouth going dry. "Mabel?" she cried, turning her head back and forth. "Mabel? Where are you?" The sound of the organ grinder drowned out her words. A little monkey darted through the crowds, holding out a hat for coins. The monkey jumped in front of Nora, but she ignored it, searching for a glimpse of Mabel's yellow bonnet.

And there it was, ducking inside the fortune-teller's booth, which had been painted a deep purple color sprinkled with glittery silver stars—just the sort of thing to attract a curious little girl. Nora dashed toward the booth. She pushed aside the curtain to see Mabel standing quite still, staring openmouthed at the imposing figure sitting behind a table. A framed certificate announced that this was Madame Lena

Sweeny, member of the fortune-tellers' guild.

"Welcome," Madame Sweeny said, in a voice like melted honey.

"We are not here for a reading," Nora Ratcliff said swiftly, taking in the fortune-teller's purple gown and feather-trimmed witch's hat.

Madame Lena Sweeny appeared not to hear. She beckoned to Mabel, who climbed into the chair opposite. Madame Sweeny reached for Mabel's left hand, clasping it between both of hers. Stretching out her swanlike neck, she bent over and gazed into Mabel's palm. Nora watched nervously as the fortune-teller studied the little hand without blinking. Then she sat up and beckoned to Nora. "Please, show me yours."

"I really didn't come in for a reading," Nora said, but she nevertheless picked up Mabel and placed the child squarely on her knees, holding out her own hand. Once again, Madame Sweeny extended her neck and gracefully lowered her head, contemplating Nora's palm. Suddenly nervous about what she might be told, Nora Ratcliff could feel her heart pounding as Madame Sweeny ran her fingers lightly across her skin.

"Does your husband have a history of magic in his family?" she murmured.

"Good heavens, no." Nora laughed nervously. "None whatsoever."

"Then this child is not yours."

"What on earth do you mean? Of course Mabel belongs to me."

Madame Sweeny lifted her gaze. "This child has magic running in her veins."

"Magic?" Nora swallowed, feeling her heart palpitations speed up.

"Strong magic," Madame Sweeny replied. "You say it doesn't come from your husband's side, and yet your palm reveals that you have not a drop of magical blood. It often skips generations, many generations, but there is no trace of witchcraft in your family line."

"My father always said we were a practical lot," Nora confirmed, "had our feet planted firmly on the ground. . . . I probably have soil running in my veins," she added, trying to make light of the conversation.

Madame Sweeny didn't smile. "Sometime in the next few years," she continued, "this little girl will show signs of her gift." She leaned forward, tapping her long pointed nails on the table. "Be aware that magic is often triggered by a keen passion, when the child is doing something she loves and feels excited about. She may start to lift off the ground," Madame Sweeny warned. "Or send objects floating around the room. Things may spark when she touches them, or change color. Magic in children is extremely unstable until they have learned to control it."

"So what do I do?" Nora questioned rather anxiously. "Having no experience with witchcraft myself."

"Watch her closely," Madame Sweeny advised in a somber voice. "She has an inquisitive nature to go with her magic, and that can be a dangerous combination."

Chapter Two

....

A Sudden Burst
of Magic

IT IS TIME WE HIRED A NANNY," NORA INFORMED DAISY that afternoon. Nora wasn't sure how she felt about Madame Sweeny's prediction, but the fortune-tellers' guild was a respectable organization, and it couldn't hurt to be prepared.

"A nanny?" Daisy said indignantly, picking up the tea tray. "Don't I do a good enough job, mam, looking after Miss Mabel? I keep her out of the greenhouse so she doesn't disturb your roses." Nora spent many hours in her greenhouse, planting and grafting and tending to her flowers. She was a keen gardener and a member of the Rose Growers' Association.

"You do a wonderful job, Daisy, but it's too much work, and Mabel is going to need watching closely from now on."

"Magic!" Daisy marveled when she heard. "That's a rare and special thing to have, mam." She glanced over at Mabel, who was sitting on the floor, dropping currants in her milk to see if they floated. Her hair ribbons had come untied, and there was sugared bun around her mouth. Daisy had a strong suspicion that the fortune-teller might perhaps have gotten it wrong. Not that Daisy had seen many witches in her life, but they did occasionally fly over Melton Bay, swooping past on their broomsticks in long, purple cloaks. They always looked so elegant and graceful, which were not words you would use in connection with Mabel.

"I shall advertise in the *Ladies' Home Journal*," Nora decided. "That will attract a suitable nanny. Someone with a great deal of experience and excellent refer-ences." And ten days later, much to Mabel's horror and Daisy's dismay, Nanny Grimshaw arrived, clutching a brown leather case and a tightly wrapped umbrella. She was thin as a fire poker. Her frizzled gray hair poked out of a crisp, white bonnet, and when she smiled, Mabel hid behind Nora's skirts because Nanny Grimshaw's eyes refused to join in.

"I keep my charges on a tight leash, Mrs. Ratcliff," Nanny Grimshaw announced, her umbrella hooked over her arm. "Mabel will be instructed in all the skills necessary to a young lady—embroidery, darning, et cetera."

"Of course," Nora agreed, deciding not to mention the possibility of Mabel being a witch. There was no need to concern Nanny about something that might never happen.

And so a new routine began in the Ratcliff residence. While Nora worked in her greenhouse, Mabel was no longer allowed to drop her shoes and handkerchiefs through the stairway banisters, seeing what landed in the hall first. She wasn't allowed to roll Daisy's pastry scraps into balls and discover if they bounced. Her hands were rubbed raw with carbolic soap because Nanny Grimshaw had a fear of germs, and her curiosity was smothered like a candle.

On the first warm afternoon, Nora suggested Nanny Grimshaw take Mabel down to the beach, insisting that the sea air was better for Mabel than a stroll in the park. Nanny Grimshaw agreed, smiling, but as they left the house her smile slipped away, and Mabel could hear her muttering, "Gritty sticky sand."

"It's fun," Mabel said, trying to get the smile to return.

"Children do not speak unless they are spoken to," Nanny Grimshaw replied.

The Cranford and Fitzwilliam children were already there, and it wasn't long before Nanny Grimshaw was deep in conversation with their nannies. She seemed to have forgotten all about Mabel, who crouched by the water, looking wistfully over at the other children as she made driftwood rafts and feather boats and sailed them out to sea. By the time Nanny Grimshaw called to her, Mabel's sunbonnet had slipped off and her petticoats and dress were soaked.

"Look at you," Nanny snapped, tying her bonnet on far too tight. "You're a disgrace, Mabel Ratcliff. Playing with dirty sticks and feathers. Your clothes are soaked. Your skin is burnt." Nanny Grimshaw pulled her roughly down the beach. "Not that I'm surprised," she hissed softly. "Now I know where you came from."

They were walking so fast, Mabel almost had to run to keep up. But as soon as they got home, Nanny Grimshaw's smile returned, the way it always did around Mabel's mother. It was like having two different Nannies in the same body, Mabel thought, except Nora always got the nice one.

"I'm afraid we're going to have to work on better listening," Nanny Grimshaw reported with a sigh. "Mabel was rather out of control."

"Oh, Mabel," Nora sighed in disappointment. "You must pay attention to Nanny."

"Sorry, Mama," Mabel whispered, wrapping her arms around Nora's legs. "I'll try harder." And Mabel did try, but it was so difficult to please Nanny Grimshaw.

One rainy day when Mabel was almost five, she sat on the sofa, practicing her embroidery. Although Mabel attempted to follow Nanny Grimshaw's directions, her fingers felt like slippery pork sausages. She kept pricking herself and tangling the thread, but Nanny Grimshaw made her sit there for two whole hours, embroidering the letter *M*.

After Mabel lost the needle down the back of the sofa, Nanny gave an exhausted sigh and declared she had one of her headaches coming on. "I am going to my room to rest, Mabel, and you will do the same." But Mabel had been sitting for so long it was difficult to lie quietly on her bed. What she wanted to do was go down to the beach and build sand castles, a tall one and a wide one, and see which the waves knocked over first. The rain pattered against the windows, and Mabel wondered if she could make a sand castle out of flour. Perhaps while Nanny napped she could try? Her mother was out in the greenhouse as usual, and

Daisy had gone into town to buy lamb chops. If Mabel cleaned up the kitchen afterward, she was sure Daisy wouldn't mind.

Being careful not to spill, Mabel dumped flour on the kitchen table. She dribbled water over it, but the mixture wouldn't stick together. Maybe she should mix sugar with water instead, Mabel thought, curious to see what would happen. Sugar felt grainy like sand, but that just made a slushy, sticky mess. By the time Daisy got back from the butcher, every surface in the kitchen was covered in white, crusty goop. And so, much to Daisy's horror, was Mabel. "If Nanny sees you like this, you are going to be in so much trouble, Miss Mabel."

"Indeed she is," Nanny Grimshaw said, standing in the doorway, her eyes narrowed and her mouth screwed into a tight knot. She made Mabel clean the table and the floor, then put her in the big tin bathtub and scrubbed her skin so hard it hurt. "No supper," Nanny pronounced, sending Mabel straight upstairs to bed. "This is not how a young lady behaves."

To stop herself from crying, Mabel thought about digging a big hole on the beach and burying Nanny in it. But the lump in her throat came back when Daisy smuggled her in some bread and jam. "Oh, Daisy, you're so nice," Mabel choked. And it grew even larger when her mother, smelling of roses and kindness, sat on the edge of Mabel's bed and gave her an extra-long good-night hug.

"Mama, Nanny is mean," Mabel whispered, burying her head against Nora's shoulder. "She holds my hand too tight and she scrubs me too hard."

"Oh, Mabel." Nora kissed her daughter on the forehead. "She holds your hand tight because she doesn't want to lose you, and you needed a good scrubbing today."

"I don't like her smile. It's not a proper one," Mabel added, which made Nora laugh.

"My nanny never smiled much when I was a little girl. Most nannies don't. That's not their job. And they have to be tough because they want us to grow up properly. It wasn't until I left the nursery that I realized I loved my nanny."

"Well, I don't love Nanny Grimshaw," Mabel whispered as Nora left the room.

A few weeks after Mabel's fifth birthday, on a hot August Saturday, Nora insisted on a trip to the beach. "I need to collect some seaweed," she told Nanny. "It's meant to be an excellent fertilizer for roses, and we can all enjoy the sea breeze."

When they arrived at the shore, the Cranford and

Fitzwilliam children were busy building a huge sand castle with turrets and a driftwood drawbridge. They had dug a deep moat around it. "To keep Mabel out!" Eliza murmured spitefully, noticing Mabel standing nearby.

"That's a nice castle," Mabel said, watching them. "I could help build it if you like. We could make it the tallest castle on the beach."

Eliza whispered something to Hettie Fitzwilliam, and the girls started giggling. "You're being a nuisance," Eliza said, swatting her shovel in Mabel's direction as if she were an annoying fly. "Go away. Nobody invited you to join in."

Mabel blinked hard to stop tears from welling up and peeled a flake of burnt skin off her nose. "Why can't I play?" she asked, unable to hide the longing in her voice.

"Because you're weird, Mabel, that's why. Licking shells, making things out of rubbish. And your mother was an earthworm." Eliza giggled. "She lived in a flowerpot!"

"My mother is not an earthworm," Mabel replied, pointing along the beach. "She's right there."

"Go away," Thomas Cranford said, copying his older sister and waving his shovel in Mabel's face. "You can't play."

Mabel looked over at Nanny Grimshaw, but she was huddled with the other nannies, talking. "I don't mind if you want to help me," Mabel said, her lip quivering. She started to dig, wondering how tall you could build a sand castle before it fell over, and decided to make her creation more of a sand tower than a castle. Mabel ran back and forth to the sea, remembering to hold up her petticoats as she filled her bucket with water. The wetter the sand the easier it was to work with, Mabel discovered, forgetting the other children. Her tower got taller and taller and began to tilt slightly to the left. It looked a bit like the Leaning Tower of Pisa, which she had seen a photograph of in one of the big encyclopedias at home. A great swell of excitement rose inside Mabel.

"That's not a proper castle," Eliza pointed out, glancing over at Mabel's structure.

"It's not meant to be a castle," Mabel explained. "It's the Leaning Tower of Melton Bay!" Her toes had started to tingle. Suddenly the sand felt too warm and her skin too sensitive. A hot, tickly sensation spread over her feet. Mabel jumped in the air, letting out a cry of surprise. She seemed to hover for a second before coming back down, and then laughed nervously, unsure what was happening. Staring at her toes, she jumped again, giving her feet a little kick. The strange, tingly feeling spread up Mabel's legs and into her stomach, fizzing its way through her chest and arms and up into her head. It was the most unusual sensation, and slowly, as if she were filling with hot air, Mabel began to rise. Her skirts billowed out and she screamed.

The children started screaming too. "Mabel's floating!" "Look at Mabel."

"Mabel Ratcliff!" Nanny Grimshaw screeched, rushing toward her charge. "Come down here this instant!" She tried to grab Mabel's foot, but couldn't reach.

"Mama," Mabel cried in alarm, scared at what was happening. She tipped forward and waved her arms about, trying to get back to the ground.

"Come here," Nora shouted, seeing the commotion and running along the beach.

"I don't know how," Mabel yelled, frantically kicking her legs. Luckily the wind was blowing in from the sea, so instead of heading out to open waters, Mabel drifted lazily toward the pier. Now that she had stopped rising, her panic began to subside.

Mr. Miller, who ran the donkey rides, was staring, openmouthed. "She's got the gift," he cried out, letting go of one of his donkeys. "Mrs. Ratcliff's girl is magic!"

"Magic!" Nanny Grimshaw gasped, gawking up at Mabel.

A slow thrill of pleasure spread through Mabel. She flapped her arms like a bird, spinning around on the gentle breeze. A pair of seagulls squawked at her, and Mabel giggled. It was the most delicious feeling, being weightless as a feather.

"I'll get you down," Nora cried, clambering over the seawall. She raced along the pier, pushing her way through the crowds. Flinging aside the curtain of the fortune-telling booth, Nora panted, "It's happened, Madame Sweeny, just like you predicted. My daughter Mabel is floating away."

Without need for further explanation, Madame Lena Sweeny rose from her chair and swept out of the tent, her full purple skirts swishing behind her. She pulled a wand from an embroidered holder fastened around her waist and pointed it at Mabel. "Collectico," she called out in a singsong voice. Immediately a spool of purple ribbon shot from her wand and flew toward Mabel, tying itself around her waist in a floppy bow. Reaching for the ribbon, Madame Sweeny gently pulled Mabel toward the pier. There was a cheer from the crowd, and Nora rushed over, Nanny Grimshaw hurrying behind.

"Wait!" Madame Sweeny raised a hand. "Don't release her. She will float right back up again." Turning to Mabel, the fortune-teller said, "You must breathe slowly, child. Ground your magic." She demonstrated for Mabel, taking in a few deep breaths and waving a hand down the length of her body. "Do you feel tingly inside?"

"Like I swallowed soap bubbles, but without the nasty taste," Mabel said.

"That's your magic," Madame Sweeny replied. "You need to center it in your belly, send it down into your feet, otherwise you're going to keep floating away." Mabel nodded, and the fortune-teller looked at Nora. "Her gift is strong, just as I predicted. She will eventually stop floating, but for the moment, I suggest you keep her tethered to the ribbon whenever you are outside, otherwise you run the risk of losing her."

"Oh my goodness." Nora put a hand to her chest. "That must not happen."

"Look," Madame Sweeny said, gesturing at Mabel. "She is already learning how to control it." Every time Mabel started to lift off the ground, she took a few deep breaths, copying what Madame Sweeny had shown her. The fortune-teller tied a loop at the end of the ribbon and held it out, but before Nora could take it, Nanny Grimshaw stepped up and grasped the ribbon firmly in her hand.

"There is a school for witches in the village of Potts Bottom," Madame Sweeny continued, "by the name of Ruthersfield. I suggest you write to Miss Brewer, the headmistress, and inquire about a place for Mabel. She needs to learn how to use her gift properly."

"I shall post a letter this afternoon," Nora said rather shakily. "Without your kind assistance, Madame Sweeny, I dread to think what would have happened to poor Mabel."

"No doubt the child would eventually have blown out to sea."

"Oh, dear me," Nora Ratcliff said, feeling quite faint. "What a dreadful thought."

"It wouldn't be the first time," Madame Sweeny said somberly.

"It's so unfair," Mabel heard Eliza whisper to Hettie. "I should have gotten the gift, not her. Witches are elegant and graceful. They don't make weird things out of rubbish or have dull names like Mabel. Eliza Anastasia Cranford. Now that's a proper name for a witch."

....

Chapter Three

Welcome to Ruthersfield

IT TOOK TWO POTS OF DAISY'S STRONGEST TEA BEFORE Nora felt back to herself. Nanny Grimshaw had retired to her room, claiming a headache due to all the excitement, and Mabel spent the rest of the afternoon floating up to the ceiling and touching the plaster molding before breathing her way back down.

"What do witches do, Mama?" Mabel asked, attempting a wobbly somersault.

"Well, they tell fortunes and make magic spells," Nora said. "Love charms, healing balms, things like that."

"And glide about looking graceful," Daisy added,

plumping up the cushions. She hugged a blue velvet pillow against her chest. "Witches are the most elegant creatures in the world."

"Do you think they make sand castles that don't wash away, or ice cream that never melts?" Mabel asked, landing on the bear rug in front of the fire. "That's what I want to do with my magic." And then in a quieter voice, "Do you think they have dull, boring names like Mabel?"

"My mother was called Mabel," Nora said rather sharply. "It's a lovely name."

"But it just doesn't sound very magical," Mabel whispered. "Couldn't I change it to something else? Like Anastasia? That is a beautiful name for a witch." Mabel yawned.

"Take a rest," Nora said, covering her daughter with a shawl. "It's been a long day."

Mabel rubbed her eyes and curled up on her side. "Mama," she murmured softly. "Eliza said my mother was an earthworm. Isn't that silly? You're not an earthworm, are you? You don't live in a flowerpot."

Feeling her legs go suddenly weak, Nora sank down on the sofa. She glanced at Daisy and said, "Of course I'm your mama, Mabel. Eliza is talking nonsense."

That evening, when Mabel was safely tucked up in bed (the ribbon tied around one of the bedposts just in case she did some nighttime floating), Nora sat down at her desk and penned a letter to the headmistress of Ruthersfield Academy, explaining the situation with Mabel. "If they offer her a place, Daisy, I have decided to leave Melton Bay," Nora said, accepting the cocoa Daisy was offering.

"But this is your home, mam. And what about all those roses you've worked so hard on growing? Trying to make them smell extra nice and bloom different colors and things." Daisy frowned and bit her lip. "Where will you go, mam?"

"I believe I shall move to Potts Bottom so Mabel will be near the academy." Nora screwed the lid on her ink pen and took a sip of cocoa. She sighed softly. "I can take plant cuttings with me, Daisy. They will put down fresh roots. But it won't be long before Eliza Cranford brings up the matter of Mabel's beginnings again. And I can't bear to see Mabel getting hurt."

"I don't mean to speak out of turn, mam, but you can't shield Miss Mabel forever." Daisy twisted her hands together. "She is bound to find out sooner or later."

"Not if we move to Potts Bottom. No one knows us there, and if I can protect my daughter from unnecessary pain, then I intend to do that." Nora's voice was hard, and Daisy lowered her eyes.

"Of course, mam."

Surprisingly, it was only six days after the letter had been sent that a reply arrived for Nora. "They would like to see Mabel for an interview," she said, informing Nanny Grimshaw. "Next Tuesday afternoon. I will accompany Mabel myself, of course, so please have her dressed in her new crinoline frock. We are to take the train to Little Shamlington, and a carriage will be waiting to escort us over to Ruthersfield."

Mabel had never ridden in a steam train before, which was exciting enough, but a day without Nanny Grimshaw was even more exciting. Nora had tied the ribbon around Mabel's waist for the trip, and she held the other end tightly in her lap.

"I can't concentrate to stay down, Mama," Mabel said, as they sped past fields and villages. "See how fast we're going! So much faster than Mr. Miller's donkeys!" She clapped her hands in delight, and wisps of purple smoke puffed out between her fingers. Mabel blinked in surprise, watching the smoke drift upward.

When they arrived in Little Shamlington, a smart purple carriage was waiting to meet them. It had the Ruthersfield crest on the side, a cauldron and two crossed broomsticks. Once Nora and Mabel were settled inside, they trundled through narrow, hedge-lined roads, Mabel's face pressed against the window. Potts Bottom was much smaller than Melton Bay, and crossing over a bridge, Mabel saw barges floating down the canal, pulled along by horses. She stared in fascination as they wove through twisty cobbled streets, past a bakery and a butcher's shop with rabbits and chickens hanging upside down in the window. Best of all Mabel liked the wooden shoe sign swaying above the cobbler's shop. The carriage slowed as they turned down Glover Lane, and the horses trotted between wide iron gates, coming to a stop in front of a large, gray, stone building.

"That's the witch school?" Mabel said, looking at Nora for confirmation.

"Yes, this is Ruthersfield," Nora murmured, checking that her hat was on straight. Holding tight to Mabel's ribbon, they walked up the broad front stairs, arriving at a handsome pair of carved double doors. Nora pulled on the bell rope, and a low clanging sounded from inside.

"Please could you call me Anastasia?" Mabel whispered, in between deep breaths.

A witch in a purple cloak opened the door. She wore a feather-and-bead-trimmed hat. Tight auburn ringlets framed her face. "Mrs. Ratcliff, I presume? And this must be?"

"Mabel," Nora said quickly, and Mabel gave a hop as two black cats sauntered past her.

"Welcome to Ruthersfield," the witch said. "I hope your journey wasn't too taxing."

"It was most pleasant, thank you," Nora replied.

"I'm Miss Seymour. I teach some of the magic hands classes here at the academy." Mabel wanted to know what magic hands classes were, but she was too shy to ask. "I know Miss Brewer is most eager to meet you, so if you'll follow me, I shall take you along to her office."

Mabel stared about the hallway. There was a plush horsehair sofa covered in what she thought at first were piles of fluffy black cushions, but which on closer inspection turned out to be sleeping cats. She wiggled her toes in her tight kidskin boots, wanting to unbutton them and slide across the smooth, polished floor in her stockings.

"Ready?" Miss Seymour said, smiling at Mabel as if she could tell what Mabel was thinking. "We don't want to keep Miss Brewer waiting."

They walked down a number of long corridors, and whenever they passed a classroom with the door open, Mabel peered inside, squinting so she could see properly. Lately, things far away had started to look a little blurry, as if there was a constant sea fog clouding her vision. Nanny Grimshaw hated it when Mabel squinted, saying if the wind changed, her face would stay that way.

"That's our cookery lab," Miss Seymour said. "The girls are making light-as-air cakes today, which calls for a cup of west wind. And west winds can be rather unruly if the girls don't mix them in quickly enough. That's why we keep the door open." Just then a strong breeze knocked Mabel to the floor and went swirling off down the corridor. "They don't like feeling trapped," Miss Seymour explained, helping Mabel to her feet.

Miss Seymour stopped in front of a green leather door. She knocked once, and a sharp voice called out, "Enter." They were ushered into Miss Brewer's office, which was filled with rugs and books and potted plants. Miss Brewer herself appeared ancient. It was impossible to tell how old she might be, except that her skin was as wrinkled as a lizard's and she wore her silver hair back in a bun. A string of jet beads dangled around her neck.

"Mrs. Ratcliff, what a pleasure," Miss Brewer said. The headmistress was sitting behind a huge walnut desk. She picked up a pair of spectacles on a long ivory handle and stared at Mabel through them. "How old are you, child?"

"Five and three quarters," Mabel whispered, not letting go of her mother's hand.

Miss Brewer raised an eyebrow, continuing to study Mabel. Finally she put her spectacles aside and flapped her hands at them. "Do sit, do sit. I have ordered some refreshment." When a maid brought in a tray loaded with tea and fruitcake, Mabel forgot her shyness and helped herself to a piece. The fruitcake was delicious and she chewed away happily, her mouth full of nuts and sugared plums. "Small bites, Mabel," Miss Brewer instructed. "It is not fitting to have such a hearty appetite. And sit up straight, child. You are slouching like a sack of onions."

The headmistress looked at Nora. "Here at Ruthersfield we pride ourselves on teaching young girls more than just the traditional skills of magic. These things are certainly important, but so are poise and manners, learning to become a gracious hostess. Each girl leaves here knowing how to dance the waft and glide, create a sparkling conversation spell, and thanks to our excellent magic hands program, all our graduates excel in the fine art of making homes more pleasant and beautiful. They will also be taught how to knit a wand case, sew a spell apron, and embroider covers for their crystal balls."

"And magic hands is a class?" Nora inquired rather nervously.

"It covers many classes. Knitting, sewing, embroidery, cookery." Miss Brewer gave a proud smile. "We even teach magic in the garden."

"I see," Nora said, glancing at her daughter. Mabel

had stopped eating and was staring at Miss Brewer in alarm. The last time Nanny Grimshaw had tried to teach her how to knit, she almost poked Nanny's eye out and managed to tie herself to the chair.

"Close your mouth, please, Mabel. It is not polite," Miss Brewer said. "Now, why don't you show me what sort of magic you can do?" She tapped a letter opener on the table. "You must understand, Mrs. Ratcliff, we have far more girls applying for places than we can possibly accommodate."

"That is why we are here, Miss Brewer. So you can judge Mabel's magic for yourself." Nora turned to Mabel. "Can you show Miss Brewer your floating?"

Mabel nodded, trying to rise into the air. But her magic wasn't fizzing the way it had been. All that talk of embroidery and knitting and not eating too much cake made her feel as leaden and heavy as a boulder.

"Relax, Mabel," Miss Brewer advised. "Think of what you were doing when you first started to float."

Mabel shut her eyes, imagining the Leaning Tower of Melton Bay. It really had been a spectacular invention, and she smiled as her toes began to tingle. The tingling spread up her legs, and Mabel felt as if she was being tickled all over from the inside. With a wisp of laughter she slowly began to rise.

"Well done," Nora encouraged as Mabel floated up

to the ceiling. She did a somersault before remembering that it wasn't polite to show her pantalets.

"That will do," Miss Brewer said, watching Mabel breathe her way back down. "You clearly have the gift, Mabel, but you need to work on your modesty." She stood up and walked over to a cupboard, returning with a crystal ball. Miss Brewer placed the ball on her desk. "This will show me the strength of your magic, so you need to focus."

Mabel sat up straight like Nanny Grimshaw had taught her, but she couldn't resist reaching out to touch the crystal ball. It reminded her of a large, beautiful marble.

"Hands off!" Miss Brewer barked, causing Mabel to jerk away. Her cheeks burned.

"I'm sorry, Miss Brewer."

"What I want you to do is think of the color blue, Mabel. Think really hard and try to turn the ball that color."

Mabel stared at the crystal, imagining a deep ocean blue. She could feel her magic starting to fizz, and much to her delight the ball began to turn color. Waves of blue swirled around the glass, and she wondered if she could make it go yellow. Mabel pictured a warm golden yellow, and with a squeal of joy she watched the ball change color again. It went from yellow to red to green as Mabel kept switching colors in her head, bouncing up and down in her chair.

"That's enough," Miss Brewer shouted, apparently not for the first time. Mabel blinked in distress, aware that she hadn't been listening. The headmistress's face was mottled, and Mabel buried her face in Nora's sleeve. Her lip trembled and she knew if Miss Brewer shouted at her again, she would cry. But when the headmistress spoke, her voice was surprisingly calm. "I asked you to stop, Mabel. Three times."

"Sorry," Mabel whispered. "I didn't hear you, Miss Brewer. I just wanted to make it change color."

"If you come to Ruthersfield, Mabel, you will learn to do as you are told. Magic is a wonderful gift, but it is not to be fooled with. Otherwise it can be very dangerous."

"Sorry," Mabel repeated, daring a look at Miss Brewer. She couldn't help noticing that the crystal ball was now a dark, muddy brown where the colors had swirled together.

"That is not blue, is it, Mabel?"

"No," Mabel whispered. "It's not." She waited for Miss Brewer to tell her what a disaster she was. How she'd never be successful as a witch.

Instead Miss Brewer sat back in her chair, making a steeple with her fingers. She looked somberly at Nora. "Mabel will need to learn to follow rules, and work on her manners. But I believe with training and discipline she has the potential to be an excellent witch." Miss Brewer broke into a smile. "And I would like to offer her a place."

"How marvelous!" Nora said, while Mabel stared at Miss Brewer in disbelief.

"The September after she turns seven we will be expecting her."

"Seven?" Nora asked. "Isn't that a little long to wait?"

"Magic in a young child is extremely unstable, which is why we don't start the teaching process sooner. By seven Mabel's magic will have settled down and she will be ready to use a wand." Leaning over her desk, Miss Brewer tapped Mabel on the knee with her glasses. "Sit up straight and get your fingers out of your mouth. Good posture is so important. You'll find that out when you learn to fly a broomstick."

"Yes, Miss Brewer," Mabel said, removing her fingers and sitting on her hands so she wouldn't be tempted to suck on them. She had a feeling they weren't going to be making things like sand castles that never washed away or ice cream that didn't melt. It seemed like such a waste, Mabel thought wistfully, to use her magic on becoming a gracious hostess, when there were so many more exciting things she'd rather do with it.

Chapter Four

....

Winifred Delacy

NOT LONG AFTER MABEL'S INTERVIEW, NORA BOUGHT a pretty fieldstone house on the outskirts of Potts Bottom, won over by some spectacular Royal Duchess roses blooming in the garden and a tiny, glass greenhouse tucked around the back. It was much less grand than the Melton Bay residence, but Mabel liked the way it felt, friendly and welcoming. Nanny Grimshaw, on the other hand, had sniffed when she first saw it and muttered that this was not at all what she had been expecting, although Daisy approved because there was less house to clean. And Nora had never been happier, planting her cuttings and trimming back the roses before she had even unpacked.

Mabel tried to make friends, but it wasn't easy with Nanny Grimshaw. She wouldn't allow Mabel to talk to the butcher's boy when he came by with his meat deliveries, saying he smelled of pig blood, had dirty clothes, and didn't pronounce his words correctly. And Mabel wasn't permitted to ride along on the milk cart with Mr. Smith and his daughter, Mary, when they invited her, because (according to Nanny) Mary smelled of sour milk, didn't brush her hair, or pronounce her words correctly either.

"Those are not suitable friends for a properly brought up young lady," Nanny Grimshaw had said. "Although I'm not surprised you would gravitate toward them," she muttered under her breath, "knowing where you came from."

"I like them because they're nice to me," Mabel said, not understanding what Nanny Grimshaw meant.

Most mornings, Mabel would work on her reading and writing, stuck away in the stuffy upstairs nursery. Her head ached as she tried to memorize the long, boring poems Nanny Grimshaw gave her to study. But the afternoons were even worse. Mabel would sit with her embroidery, pricking holes in her thumb as she listened to the clock tick away the hours, dreaming of all the things she wasn't allowed to do. Occasionally Nanny Grimshaw would nod off to sleep and then, if she were feeling daring, Mabel would creep over to the bookcase and read some of Dr. Ratcliff's books, learning about astronomy and steam power and all sorts of fascinating discoveries. This was always risky though, because if Nanny Grimshaw woke up and discovered Mabel away from her embroidery, she was forced to sit for another hour.

That whole first year in Potts Bottom, magic fizzed out of Mabel. Ladybugs turned purple when they landed on her arm, and sometimes, when she was eating, her fork would fly out of her hand and spin about the room. One day, staring at a picture of a Ferris wheel in the newspaper, Mabel got so excited, thinking of a huge wheel that spun around with people on board, her fingers started to tingle and the paper began to smoke. Luckily, Daisy managed to grab it out of Mabel's hands and throw it through the window right before it burst into flames.

By the time Mabel turned seven she finally stopped floating and her magic had begun to calm down. She was able to control it more now. Mabel discovered that by waving her fingers in circles she could stir up little winds, and if she rubbed leaves between her hands, they grew rubbery and soft. One day, catching sight of Mabel stretching leaves into different shapes, Nanny Grimshaw had grabbed her by the ear and barked, "You're not supposed to be playing with your magic. Your mother won't be pleased when I tell her."

"Better wait till you start school," Nora said gently, when she heard what Mabel had been up to. "Remember what Miss Brewer told us? Magic can be dangerous if you don't know what you're doing."

But once Mabel began at Ruthersfield, she found out rather quickly that most of their time was spent in magic hands class, or dance class, or practicing the correct way to hold a crystal ball. "Long, willowy necks, girls," their fortune-telling teacher, Miss Regan, commanded, making Mabel feel like an overheated turtle as she stretched up her head, trying to remember to keep a straight back. Mabel's hands always got so hot and sweaty, and she couldn't flutter her fingertips in the graceful way that Miss Regan demonstrated.

The girls were not allowed to experiment with their magic. At all. Something Mabel discovered during her first potions class. They had been instructed to mix up small sachets of smelling salts, which were essential to have on hand because students were always swooning in the hallways, often when the toads escaped from the spells and charms room. But in place of crushed butterfly wings, Mabel mixed a hyena laugh into her salts, curious to see what would happen. And when she waved them under Cynthia Price's nose (who had fainted at the sight of a toad), poor Cynthia came round braying with laughter instead of fluttering her eyes open in the ladylike fashion that the butterfly wings ensured. Distraught at the noise she was making, Cynthia promptly collapsed again.

"I'm really sorry," Mabel apologized to Miss Mantel, the potions teacher. "I just thought it might make the girls feel more cheerful when they woke up."

"Meddling about with magic is not part of this curriculum," Miss Mantel replied crisply. "We are a school of traditions. You will follow the spells precisely as they are written. Remind me of your name, please, girl?"

"Magnolia," Mabel whispered, before she could stop herself.

"Magnolia?" Miss Mantel frowned, knowing this didn't sound quite right. "Please report for cobweb-sweeping duty after school then, Magnolia."

Mabel blushed hotly, realizing it wouldn't take Miss Mantel long to find out the truth. In fact, it took her less than two minutes before she remembered Mabel's real name, and poor Mabel had to write out "I will not lie to my teacher" fifty times, on top of cobweb-sweeping duty. Luckily none of the girls who had overheard made fun of her. In fact, much to Mabel's surprise, they were most sympathetic, huddling around her after class.

"You can always change your name when you grow up," Tabitha Pritchard said. "I think you look like a Rosamalinda."

"Or a Crystabella," Lucy Habersham suggested. "I've always loved the name Crystabella. It reminds me of a princess."

"I wish there was a spell that would make people forget I was called Mabel," Mabel sighed. "So when people spoke to me they'd say 'hello, Magnolia,' and dull old 'Mabel' would be erased from their minds. Nobody would ever call me that again."

"Well, I like the name, Mabel," Ruby Tanner said softly. She was a thin, pale girl with even thinner, paler hair. "It's a strong, capable name." And Mabel tried to remind herself of this every time her wand case ended up in tangles, or as she struggled to master the waft and glide.

Curiosity burned inside her like an oil lamp, glowing dimmer and dimmer in the stifling atmosphere, but never completely going out. Nothing could extinguish Mabel's longing to experiment, turning a spell inside out to see what would happen or giving an extra little flick with her wand. Which is why she ended up on cobweb-sweeping duty more times during her first term than any other girl in the school. But however constricting Mabel found Ruthersfield to be, for the first time in her life she had friends. Lots and lots of friends. There was nothing more wonderful than sitting at the lunch table with a whole group of girls, laughing and chattering away, and Mabel soon became known for her spontaneous hugs. She would fling her arms around girls in the hallway, slipping squares of Daisy's homemade toffee into their pockets.

There was only one girl Mabel couldn't seem to make friends with. And that was Winifred Delacy, or Lady Winifred Delacy as she constantly reminded her classmates. Winifred wore her hair in fat gold ringlets and pranced around school as if she were already in year twelve, and not just a first former. Her father was Lord Winthrop Delacy the third, one of the biggest landowners in the county. He was on the board of governors at Ruthersfield, a fact that Winifred brought up regularly. Mabel had only spoken about a dozen words with Winifred since starting at the academy, and she had a strong suspicion they wouldn't be exchanging many more after Mabel had accidently wobbled into her and knocked Winifred to the ground during dance class. Winifred had left the studio limping dramatically, supported by Diana Mansfield and Florence Steiner, her two chosen friends.

"She's not really hurt," Ruby said. "She's just pretending to make you look bad."

"Why?" Mabel asked, sounding baffled.

"Because you showed her up in spell chanting class last week. Not that you meant to," Ruby added quickly. "But didn't you hear Miss Wiggins call her a growler? Right after she said you chanted like a songbird! And you do have a lovely chanting voice."

"Oh!" Mabel groaned. "So that's the reason Winifred's been giving me mean looks. If only I'd knocked you over. You wouldn't have minded, Ruby. Why did I have to bump into Winifred? Now she's really going to hate me."

Things got even worse one Monday when Miss Heathcliff, their spells and charms teacher, called on Winifred to demonstrate in class. "Now, today," Miss Heathcliff began, "we will be practicing a glamorizing spell, one of the oldest spells in the history of witchcraft." She smiled at the class and said, "Something you will all be using when it's time to find a husband." There were some giggles from the girls, and Miss Heathcliff continued, "So we're going to practice 'glamorizing' on this lovely creature." She picked up a large, lumpy toad from one of the glass terrariums at the back of the classroom. A number of the girls squealed and covered their faces, but Mabel leaned over her desk, trying to get a better look. "This is a complex spell, and as first-year students you will be practicing the first step only, making the skin of Mr. Toad here all smooth and glossy, instead of this lumpy, warty surface he has now. Well, come on, Winifred," Miss Heathcliff said, beckoning her up to the front of the class. "No dillydallying."

"Winifred, you'll be great at this," her friend Diana Mansfield whispered. "You know all about elegance and charm."

Miss Heathcliff placed the toad on her table. "Now, what you have to do, Winifred, is point your wand at him and with three graceful flicks, chant out, 'Glamaricious!'"

Winifred moistened her lips. Holding up her wand, she gave it three quick flicks, and in a rather quivery voice, called out, "Glamaricious!" There was a puff of mauve smoke, and when it cleared, Mabel saw that half the toad's back was a smooth velvety green and the other half appeared to be covered in enormous lumpy warts, three times the size of the original bumps. Some of the girls snickered, and Winifred glared at Mabel, which Mabel felt was quite unfair because she hadn't been making the noise.

"You need to practice your wand control, Winifred," Miss Heathcliff said crisply. She pointed at Mabel. "Your turn, Mabel Ratcliff. And don't try to give him fur or wings or anything else you might be thinking about. Just follow the spell as instructed, please."

Ruby gave her an encouraging nod, and Mabel walked to the front of the class. She waited a moment while Miss Heathcliff undid Winifred's attempt. The toad didn't seem to mind. He sat quite patiently, blinking every now and then. Taking a deep breath and concentrating on the spell, Mabel waved her wand at the toad, giving three little flicks and just managing to stop herself from adding a fourth flick to see what might happen. There was the cloud of mauve smoke, but this time when it cleared, the whole class *oohed* because the skin of Mabel's toad was smooth as butter and a glorious, shiny green.

"Beautiful job, Mabel," Miss Heathcliff exclaimed.

"Well done, Mabel," Lucy Habersham called out.

Mabel couldn't stop beaming, until she realized that Winifred was scowling at her. "You're such a show-off, Mabel," she hissed, as Mabel walked back to her seat. "Thinking you're so popular. How dare you make me look bad and laugh at me."

"But I wasn't," Mabel whispered, losing all the joy of her success. Winifred turned away, and Mabel was left with the uncomfortable feeling that Lady Winifred Delacy was not someone who forgave easily.

Chapter Five

....

An Interesting Discovery

IT WAS AMAZING TO MABEL THAT WINIFRED DELACY
could carry on a feud for four straight years, but that
is exactly what happened. Mabel tried her hardest to
be friendly, but she quickly realized that Winifred had
no intention of being nice to her, and the best course of
action was to stay out of her way. Occasionally, Mabel
caught Winifred sneaking glances at her paper during
a test, or copying what she was doing in potions class
(which wasn't always a good idea), but Winifred would
never actually ask Mabel for help. Or say thank you
for letting her copy.

"She's a cheat," Ruby said after a geography test

one day. "I saw her looking at your paper, Mabel. Why don't you tell the teacher?"

"Because then Winifred would hate me even more," Mabel sighed.

Sometimes Mabel couldn't make up her mind who was worse, Winifred Delacy or Nanny Grimshaw. Actually, that was easy, because for the most part she could ignore Winifred. And ignoring Nanny Grimshaw was not an option, unless it was Sunday, Nanny's day off, and Mabel's favorite time of the week. Not only was she released from Nanny's clutches, she got to spend the entire eight hours with her mother. It was also Daisy's day off, which she usually devoted to drinking tea and reading all about her favorite stage actress, Nellie Glitters, in the magazine *Musical Monthly*.

"I adore Sundays," Mabel said one weekend afternoon, a few weeks past her eleventh birthday. She was in the garden, watching Nora brush pollen from a little linen bag onto the Royal Duchess roses. Her mother did this every year, collecting the pollen from the wild roses that ran along the hedgerows. They had a much more powerful fragrance than the Royal Duchesses, which looked beautiful but had hardly any scent, and Nora was hoping to cross-pollinate the plants. She'd learned all about it at one of the meetings of the Rose Growers' Association.

"There!" Nora put down her paintbrush and sniffed. "Definitely more fragrant this summer," she said, smiling in satisfaction. "Now, time for a nice cup of tea."

They sat at the table in the garden, and Mabel wriggled her toes in delight. She held a cherry tart in one hand and was pouring over the *Potts Bottom Gazette*, something Nanny Grimshaw never let her do. Newspapers were not for children, Nanny Grimshaw had said firmly, the first time she saw Mabel pick one up.

"Mama, look at this," Mabel said, dropping crumbs on the paper as she crammed her mouth full of tart.

"Smaller bites, please, Mabel, and don't talk with your mouth full."

Mabel swallowed and said, "They're inventing a flying machine so that nonmagical people will be able to fly too. Isn't that amazing, Mama? Almost as amazing as electricity!" Last week Mabel had read about a powerful new form of energy that could light a house at the flick of a switch and been so excited by the idea, she had hidden the article under her mattress. "I wish we could use our magic to invent things like that," Mabel sighed, reaching for another tart. "Imagine a rocket broomstick that could fly to the moon. Wouldn't that be wonderful?"

"Perhaps classes will get a little more interesting now

that you're an Intermediate Witch," Nora said, giving Mabel a sympathetic smile. She knew that magic hands and crystal ball gazing weren't Mabel's favorite subjects. And even Nora had to admit that learning love charms, or mastering the art of a "sparkling conversation" spell so you could converse with difficult guests at a dinner party, did seem rather outdated these days.

"First broomstick flying lesson on Wednesday," Mabel said with a shiver. "I'm excited about that. And nervous!" She felt around under the newspaper and pulled out a slim purple booklet. "It will be fun to fly myself to school, though. Only three more days of having to be chaperoned."

It was a strict Ruthersfield rule that all girls too young to fly must be accompanied to school and back by a twelfth former.

"Do you know the handbook?" Nora asked, helping herself to a cucumber sandwich. "Miss Brewer made it quite clear that no girl would be allowed on a broomstick unless she has memorized the Ruthersfield flying rules."

"I think so. Can you test me?" Mabel handed the booklet to Nora. Reaching for the last cherry tart, Mabel began, "A witch must always be accompanied by her cat. No flying above the tree lines. No overtaking birds. No acrobatics or reckless steering. A witch must wear her hat at all times outside the academy. A witch must keep both hands on the broomstick and keep her shoes in her skirt loops. Ummm . . ." Mabel paused a moment. "Oh, I know, don't tell me. . . . No shouting or eating allowed while flying. And most important of all, a ladylike posture must be retained at all times."

"Well done, Mabel. You have an excellent memory."

"I bet I get it from Papa," Mabel said. "Doctors need to remember all those difficult-sounding diseases and long words, don't they?"

Nora got up and started to put the tea things back on the tray, stacking the plates and gathering spoons without looking at Mabel. "Can you take this through to the kitchen, Mabel? It's getting a little cool out here."

"Of course." Mabel licked her sticky fingers. She had a feeling that her mother still missed her father more than she admitted, because whenever Mabel mentioned him, Nora always changed the subject. Which was really rather hard since there was so much Mabel wanted to know. What his favorite foods were. The sort of things he found funny. Whether he felt excited when he found out he was going to be a father. "How old was I when Papa got the influenza?" Mabel asked softly. She wanted to know if her father got to hold her as a baby, but there never seemed to be a right time for such a question, especially when her mother was so good at avoiding all conversations about Mabel's birth.

"Frank died before you were born," Nora said, picking up her shears from the grass. She gave Mabel a bright smile. "I must prune back the climbing roses," she murmured. "They are getting quite out of control."

Mabel let the subject drop. But the following morning, while Nanny Grimshaw was still upstairs, Mabel tried asking Daisy some questions. Like which of her parents she had resembled as a baby? Daisy just shooed her away from the stove and said to stop pestering her, because she needed to get going on the porridge. Nanny insisted on porridge three times a week, saying it was good for the digestion, and if Mabel left any of the lumpy, slimy gruel in her bowl, Daisy had been instructed by Nanny to serve it up again for her breakfast the next day.

"Porridge!" Mabel groaned.

"Oh, here." Daisy buttered a slice of bread and handed it to Mabel. "Take this outside before Nanny sees. And don't say I gave it to you," she added, as Mabel escaped into the garden.

Letting out a long sigh, Mabel wondered why grown-ups were so good at avoiding questions. She took off her glasses and cleaned them on her skirt. The sun was bright this morning, showing up the smudges on her lenses. Not long after moving to Potts Bottom, Mabel had started bumping into things, and her squint got so bad that Nora finally took her to see the ophthalmologist over in Little Shamlington. He had recommended glasses, and all at once her surroundings took on a whole new focus. Everything became crystal clear and sharp edged, and Mabel still took delight in the clarity of the world around her, right down to counting the hairs on Nanny Grimshaw's chin. It was like stepping out of a pea soup fog.

She bent down to examine a cobweb, each tiny thread sparkling with drops of dew like crystal beads. They had been studying cobwebs in potions class, a common ingredient in many type of spells—healing balms, sleeping drafts, comfort cookies—but what fascinated Mabel the most was reading about cobwebs in the big leather encyclopedia her mother kept in the drawing room. Apparently some webs, depending on the spider that had made them, were remarkably strong, and that got Mabel thinking. Spider silk was so fine and light. What if she could find a way to strengthen it further, make it unbreakable, but keep the weight the same? There would be so many amazing uses for thread that strong and light. It would make an almost invisible net that could carry hundreds of pounds in weight, or a rope that could hold a mountaineer but take up no space in a pocket and weigh almost nothing.

Mabel sighed and stared out across the garden. She had hundreds of ideas buzzing in her head, and nowhere for them to go. The sky was so blue this morning, so full of possibilities, and a sharp longing pierced her. Knowing how much trouble she could get in, but unable to stop herself, Mabel reached into her pinafore pocket and pulled out the glass vial of extra-strength repair potion they had made last week in class. It was supposed to be used to mend broken china. You sprinkled the potion over your shattered plate or vase and the china magically repaired itself. After Mabel had mended the broken cow creamer Miss Mantel had given her, she added a tiny puff of lion's roar to the rest of her mixture, interested to see what might happen. Now, taking the lid off the vial, she sprinkled some drops over the cobweb and waited a few seconds. Then touching the web with a stick, Mabel was surprised to find it didn't break. She dropped the stick on the web and it bounced back up. With a rush of excitement Mabel carefully peeled the cobweb off the grass and stretched it. The threads still held, but its texture had changed. She pulled and pulled, and the web continued to expand as if it were made out of rubber.

"Fascinating," Mabel murmured, shoving her glasses up her nose. She wasn't sure what she had done exactly, but the results were certainly interesting. "Ouch!" Mabel cried, feeling the curved end of Nanny Grimshaw's umbrella hook under her armpit. With another loud "ouch!" she was yanked to her feet.

Nanny Grimshaw looked her up and down. "Your pinafore is dirty, your braids need tidying, and you have crumbs around your mouth. You are a disgrace, Mabel Ratcliff. Is this how we dress for school?"

"No, Nanny, sorry, Nanny."

"You have ten minutes to eat breakfast and make yourself presentable before your chaperone group comes by. Now, get going," Nanny Grimshaw said, giving Mabel a smack on the bottom with her umbrella.

Chapter Six

· ·

The Problem with Liver

THERE WERE SEVEN SENIOR STUDENTS WHO HAD THE privilege of being Ruthersfield chaperones. These girls got to fly around the streets of Potts Bottom and collect all the young witches on their route. Every morning and afternoon, the chaperones could be seen flying sedately along, trailing a line of little girls behind them. They were not allowed to fly more than two feet off the ground or go any faster than the front walker. And the twelfth former on Mabel's route was the "perfect" Violet Featherstone. Like the rest of the upper class, she wore her skirts down past her ankles and pinned up her hair. But it was the corsets the twelfth formers were obliged to wear that Mabel dreaded the most. This torturous undergarment squeezed your stomach in so tightly it was difficult to breathe. It was a well-known Ruthersfield fact that the twelfth formers competed with each other to see who had the smallest waist. That's why they were constantly fainting, Mabel thought, because they couldn't get enough air into their lungs. And it must make broomstick riding so uncomfortable. Not that you would ever guess this if you saw Violet Featherstone. She took great pride in perching sideways on her broomstick, her legs pressed together and her shoulders pulled back. Even her cat had impressive riding posture, his hind paws tucked under and his tail flagpole straight.

"No running," Violet said, as Mabel came dashing out of her house. "And put your hat on, please."

"Yes, Violet," Mabel panted, pulling on her hat as she joined the end of the line behind her friend Tabitha.

From somewhere close by a bell started ringing, and Mabel turned just in time to see their magic hands teacher barrel past on one of the big two-wheeled contraptions she had read about in the newspaper but never actually seen before. Wind blew in Mabel's face and a fizz of excitement rushed through her. "Look, a bicycle!" she shouted, as Miss Seymour sped by, curls blowing in her face, her long purple cloak streaming out behind. Mabel was so busy staring at the huge metal machine that she stumbled into Tabitha. "Sorry!" Mabel apologized, watching their teacher wobble and swerve her way down Trotting Hill. "I just can't believe Miss Seymour's riding a bicycle!"

None of the girls had seen such a sight before, and Violet Featherstone landed shakily on the pavement, her mouth dropping open in shock. Pulling some smelling salts out of her pocket and waving them under her nose, she gawked at Miss Seymour.

"Where's her broomstick?" one of the year-two witches squealed. "Why isn't she flying to school?" Most mornings Miss Seymour would pass Mabel's chaperone group, but never on a bicycle. In fact, as far as Mabel knew, this was the first bicycle sighting in Potts Bottom.

Dashing out of line, Mabel began to run down the hill. She had to see that machine up close, examine what happened when the pedals were pushed. It was like a mechanical horse that didn't need feeding, and Mabel wondered how fast it could go.

"Mabel Ratcliff," Violet called out, not raising her voice but making it clear enough and loud enough for Mabel to stop in her tracks. "Two demerits for disruptive behavior." Violet pointed her wand at Mabel, and two black Xs flew through the air, attaching themselves to the front of Mabel's pinafore. "One more this week and you will find yourself in Miss Brewer's office," Violet cautioned. Mabel swallowed the retort that was trying to escape from her mouth. She'd only get another demerit if she spoke back to Violet, and she could question Miss Seymour about her bicycle later.

"Sorry about your demerits," Tabitha said, holding her hand out to Mabel as they walked. "This will make you feel better. Quickly," she whispered, "before Violet sees."

"Chocolate?" Mabel gasped, taking the smooth brown square.

"My papa always brings me a bar back when he goes down to London on business."

"Oh, Tabitha, thank you. You are the nicest person. I only get it at Christmas as a special treat." Mabel sniffed the thick square, breathing in the sweet, chocolaty aroma. "I shall save this for after lunch."

"To take away that nasty liver taste," Tabitha said, shuddering in agreement. Every Monday they had liver, a day when the girls sat in miserable silence, staring at slabs of dense, evil-flavored organ meat lying on their plates. It was a Ruthersfield rule that you couldn't leave the table until your plate was clean, so Monday lunchtimes were always the longest in the week, with tears and groans and enough leftovers to feed all the school cats. "I hate liver." Tabitha gagged.

"It is the most disgusting, foul-tasting food in the whole world, and it should be illegal to serve it to children."

"Ruby always gets sick after Monday lunch," Mabel said. "Would you mind if I gave this chocolate to her, Tabitha? I think she hates liver even more than I do."

"I wish liver tasted like chocolate," Tabitha sighed. "Wouldn't that be marvelous?"

Mabel didn't answer. Her mind had drifted off the way it always did whenever she was thinking about one of her ideas. The girls were used to it, and Mabel made little muttering noises as she walked. It was only as they climbed up the steps into school that she slid her arm through Tabitha's and said, as if there had been no break in the conversation, "I think I can do it!"

"Do what?" Tabitha asked, looking puzzled.

"Make liver taste like chocolate." Mabel gave an animated little skip. "Remember the taste enhancer potion we made last week?"

"A hostess's best friend." Tabitha mimicked Miss Mantel's voice. "When you want your meals to sparkle and your dinner party to be the talk of the town, use taste-enhancing potion to give food that magical lift."

"Yes, and those plain boiled potatoes we sprinkled it on in class were delicious," Mabel said. "The most potatoey potatoes I've ever eaten. Like you could taste the rain and the sun and . . ."

"Mabel, where are you going with this?" Tabitha said nervously, as they walked toward the fortune-telling room.

"If I melt chocolate with the taste enhancer powder, stir it into wishing well water, which makes an excellent base solution, and then drizzle it over the liver"—Mabel paused a moment and gave another excited skip—"it should make the liver taste of chocolate."

"You know you're not allowed to experiment," Tabitha whispered. "You'll get in so much trouble."

"I won't because the teachers will never know. They'll be happy because we'll eat all our liver, and we'll be happy because the liver will taste like chocolate."

"You are mad," Tabitha said. "Completely crazy. Totally insane." And then looking around to make sure no one was listening, she asked, "Do you really think it will work?"

"I don't see why not. We've already made the taste enhancing powder and that's the hard part. I'll just mix it all together at the end of potions class."

"Which is right before lunch," Tabitha said with a grin. "The girls are going to love this!"

Luckily, in potions class they were using cauldrons to make unicorn milk soap, guaranteed to give you a soft, milky complexion, and since Mabel finished early, she was able to rinse out her cauldron and mix up her liver potion without Miss Mantel noticing.

"I thought we were only meant to use a pinch of enhancer," Ruby whispered, watching Mabel liberally sprinkle powder over the tiny puddle of melted chocolate.

"This is liver we're talking about, not potatoes," Mabel said. "It's going to need a great deal more enhancing."

Mabel and Ruby cleaned up as fast as they could and managed to make it into the dining room ahead of most classes. One group of year-four girls was already there, sitting at a table, glumly staring at their plates of liver.

"Poor things," Mabel whispered. "If only they had come in a little later."

When they got to the head of the line, Mabel waited until Mrs. Bainbridge, the cook, had turned her back for a moment to stir a pot of peas, and then quickly, before she noticed, Mabel poured her homemade potion all over the liver. There was a hissing noise, and a cloud of brown steam rose from the pan.

"Smells delicious," Mabel said, as Mrs. Bainbridge turned around. She gave Mabel a suspicious glare. The girls behind her smothered their giggles, and Mabel guessed that Tabitha had been spreading the word.

"Smells like it always smells," Mrs. Bainbridge said, scooping a large piece onto Mabel's plate. "Like liver."

Except as Mabel lifted the plate to her nose, a lovely chocolaty waft of steam blew into her face. She carried her lunch to an empty table and sat down. Ruby and Tabitha followed. Mabel sliced off a tiny corner of liver and put it cautiously between her teeth. The other girls watched as Mabel closed her eyes for a moment and moaned softly. "It's delicious," she said. "Really delicious." Warm, creamy chocolate flooded her mouth, and Mabel laughed in delight. "The best thing I've ever eaten." Not hesitating, she cut a large chunk of liver and shoved it into her mouth.

"Oh, it is so good," Ruby sighed, nibbling a piece off her fork. She looked around the dining room, sounding panicky. "I hope there's going to be enough for seconds." Picking the liver up in her hands, Ruby started gulping it down.

"Mabel, this is amazing," Tabitha gushed, forking up liver as fast as she could. "I can't stop eating it." Her cheeks bulged like a hamster's.

Groans of pleasure filled the dining hall as girls gobbled down their liver at alarming speed. Lucy Habersham was hunched over her plate, licking up chocolate juice.

"What is going on?" Miss Seymour cried out,

watching Winifred grab a piece of liver out of Diana's hands. Nancy Cox stole the last piece off her best friend, Emily's, plate, and turned away to eat it before Emily could snatch it back.

"Sit down at once," Miss Reed, the flying teacher, barked, pushing aside her plate of chicken. The teachers had a separate menu on Mondays—all except for Miss Lyons, who taught palm reading, and was one of the only people in the school who actually liked liver. Miss Lyons had shoved back her chair and was making a mad dash toward the food line.

"Seconds," Charlotte Monroe screamed, charging after Miss Lyons. There was a scraping of chairs, and a stampede of girls suddenly hurtled toward the counter.

Most of the teachers had reached for their smelling salts, while Miss Brewer banged her cane on the floor over and over again. "Will you stop this right now!" Her face was puce colored and her mouth still moved, but there was so much noise in the dining hall it was difficult to hear what she was saying.

The big metal tray that was now empty of liver clattered to the floor, and girls elbowed each other out of the way, getting down on their knees and slurping up the juice. When the last fleck of liver had been sucked, chewed, and licked out of sight, a shameful hush settled over the room.

Mabel's palms were damp, and a sick dread sloshed in her stomach. "I'm not quite sure what happened," she murmured.

"Don't say a word," Tabitha hissed. "Do not confess, Mabel."

"We're in this together," Ruby agreed, touching her friend's arm.

"Winifred won't be. If she knows it's me, she's bound to tell."

Miss Brewer stood on the teacher's podium, looking around at the girls. When she spoke, her voice was tight with anger. Words ricocheted around the hall like pistol bullets. "Would someone care to explain what just happened? Because however good a cook Mrs. Bainbridge is, I don't think her liver can be responsible for causing a riot."

None of the girls spoke, although Winifred cleared her throat rather loudly and gave Mabel a pointed look.

"It tasted of the most delicious chocolate," Miss Lyons explained, walking back to her seat. She bowed her head in embarrassment as she passed Miss Brewer. "I do apologize for my behavior."

"If the girl or girls responsible for this don't own up, the whole school will receive a punishment," Miss Brewer announced. There was some whispering, but still no one spoke.

Mabel sighed and got to her feet, "It was me, Miss Brewer. I did it."

"What a surprise, Mabel Ratcliff." Miss Brewer pinned her hawklike eyes on Mabel, and said, "Follow me to my office."

·······························

Chapter Seven

Like Mother, Like Daughter

"WOULD YOU CARE TO EXPLAIN WHAT JUST HAPPENED out there?" Miss Brewer said, studying Mabel from across her desk.

"I . . ." Mabel swallowed, not quite knowing how to begin. The silence stretched out, and Mabel could hear the grandfather clock ticking in the corner of the room, and the sound of Oscar, Miss Brewer's cat, licking his paws.

"Let me help you," Miss Brewer said at last. "You were experimenting, Mabel. Again." Mabel nodded guiltily, and Oscar yawned. "You were doing what you know is against the rules. And it is against the rules because?" Miss Brewer paused, raising her eyebrows, her jaw clenched tight.

"It's dangerous," Mabel finished.

"Yes, indeed. Something I remember making quite clear at your interview all those years ago. And a subject we have talked about many times since. It is dangerous to experiment," Miss Brewer rasped, "when you don't know what you're doing."

"I didn't mean for that to happen," Mabel said. "It was just taste enhancer powder and chocolate, but I think I put too much taste enhancer in."

Miss Brewer frowned. "Taste enhancer is an extremely safe potion. If you used a whole bottle, it would not have had that effect. There must have been something else in there."

"Only wishing well water, that's all."

"Wishing well water?" Miss Brewer snapped, leaning forward so the folds of skin on her neck trembled.

"It makes a good mixing solution," Mabel whispered. "We've used it before."

"Not with taste enhancer you haven't. Honestly, Mabel. It made the girls desperate for more. They were wishing for another bite before they had even swallowed the first. Do you have any idea how stupid that was?" Miss Brewer gave a sigh of frustration.

"I do now," Mabel said, looking at the rug. "I'm really sorry, Miss Brewer."

"You will spend the rest of the day polishing my crystal balls, Mabel, and tomorrow I ask that you stay home from school."

"Am I suspended?" Mabel asked, her voice starting to shake. Only the worst, most disobedient students ever got suspended.

"For one day," Miss Brewer said. "I will write a note to your mother, explaining the situation. Look on it more as a day of reflection rather than a day of punishment. You are a smart girl, Mabel," she added in a softer voice. "If you would just stick to the rules."

Mabel nodded, unable to speak. Her words couldn't get past the lump in her throat. Sunlight streamed through the window, and Mabel blinked back tears, watching the dust motes float about the room. A deep sadness swelled inside her. It wasn't just the shame of being suspended. It was knowing that she could never do the things she wanted with her magic. Years of making sparkling conversation spells, knitting wand cases, and perfecting the waft and glide stretched in front of her, and even though Mabel wasn't wearing a corset, the tightness in her chest was so constricting she could hardly breathe.

"Why did you do it, Mabel?" Miss Brewer asked softly. "What was the point of all that?"

"To make the liver taste nice," Mabel said, meeting Miss Brewer's gaze.

"Then why not just put it on your own meal? Why get the whole school involved?"

"Because everyone hates liver. And I thought the girls would like it."

Miss Brewer reached out a hand to stroke Oscar. "You don't have to buy the girls' friendship with clever tricks, Mabel. You have enough to offer on your own."

Mabel spent the rest of the afternoon polishing all Miss Brewer's crystal balls. Oscar jumped into her lap for company, and his soft, warm presence had a calming effect. It was only when the bell rang at the end of classes that Mabel's anxiety returned. Miss Brewer handed her a letter to give to Nora, and as Mabel got up to leave, she said, "Remember what I told you earlier, Mabel. Look on it as a day of reflection."

"Suspended!" Ruby and Tabitha gasped, crowding around Mabel in the hallway.

"Suspended," Emily Bisset repeated, overhearing as she walked by. "Mabel Ratcliff's been suspended!"

"Oh, poor Mabel."

"That's terrible."

Word spread like dragon fire, and Mabel had never felt so embarrassed as she shuffled over to join her chaperone group.

"I'm surprised they didn't expel her," Winifred said loudly. "It won't be long before Mabel gets thrown out."

"Take no notice," Tabitha said, standing protectively in line behind Mabel. Ruby gave her a quick hug before darting off to join her own chaperone group. Even Violet Featherstone gave Mabel a sympathetic look. The walk home was quiet. Violet flew slowly at the head of the line, and no one spoke.

When Mabel was dropped off, she ran straight to the greenhouse and handed the letter to her mother, wanting to avoid Nanny Grimshaw. Mabel stood in silence while Nora read. She could feel blood pulsing in her ears, and the smell of roses was overpowering. "Are you furious?" Mabel whispered at last.

"I'm disappointed that you've been suspended," Nora said. "But I'm not cross that you like to experiment, Mabel. Just not with magic, not at school." Nora sighed and tucked a strand of Mabel's hair that had escaped from one of her braids back behind her ear. "You have to follow the rules. Help me in the greenhouse if you want to experiment. We can work together."

"But I'm a witch, Mama. I want to experiment with magic," Mabel said, and to her horror she started to cry. "I'm not being bad. I just like to invent things." Her glasses fogged up, and she took them off, wiping them clean on her skirt. "None of the other girls feels like this. They don't care about experimenting. That's why they don't get into trouble." Mabel kicked at a piece of broken flowerpot. "I wish I was like everyone else, then I wouldn't care either."

"No, you don't." Nora gave a wistful smile. "But it's not easy being different. I should know." Mabel hadn't thought of her mother as different before. She was just her mama, but now that Nora mentioned it, Mabel could see she wasn't like other people's mothers, sitting in the house all day embroidering and entertaining friends. "I must say I think chocolate-flavored liver is rather ingenious," Nora said, kissing the tip of Mabel's nose.

"Nanny wouldn't approve," Mabel sighed. "She won't let me have supper, breakfast, or lunch when she hears."

"This doesn't concern Nanny," Nora said rather briskly. "It concerns you, me, and Miss Brewer. I will tell Nanny you are not going to school tomorrow, and that will be the end of the discussion."

Chapter Eight

· ·

Black Cats and Broomsticks

NANNY GRIMSHAW INSISTED THAT MABEL WORK ON HER
embroidery the following day. "You may not be
going to school, but idleness is never to be encouraged."
Daisy knew the truth because Mabel couldn't hide it
from her, and she made Mabel's favorite treacle tart
for lunch. Except Nanny wouldn't let her eat any of
it, saying if Mabel wasn't up for school, she certainly
wasn't up for treacle tart. Nora had a big meeting of the
Rose Growers' Association on Wednesday, so she spent
most of the morning working in her greenhouse, and all
afternoon writing at her desk. It was such a long, lonely
day that Mabel couldn't wait for it to be over.

Walking back into school after her suspension wasn't nearly as bad as Mabel had imagined. She thought everyone would be whispering and pointing at her, but most of the girls in Mabel's class were chattering away about their first flying lesson, which would take place immediately following attendance. Apart from a few sympathetic looks, things seemed just like they always did.

"We all still think it was a good idea," Tabitha whispered as the girls made their way out to the flying field.

"And the liver was delicious," Ruby said, "although I couldn't eat a bite of anything right now, I'm so nervous."

Miss Reed, the flying teacher, had a fierce reputation. They had been instructed to assemble under the large oak tree where Miss Reed would hand out the cats and broomsticks, and a whoosh of anticipation surged through Mabel when she saw all the broomsticks leaned up against the tree, with their smooth, polished handles and thick, new bristles. A number of black cats sat around licking their paws and grooming themselves, and a soft purring filled the air like the quiet hum of bees.

The girls jostled against each other, and Mabel accidently stepped on the soft, polished leather of

Winifred Delacy's left shoe. Winifred poked Mabel in the side. "Stop," she hissed without moving her lips. "Idiot. You shouldn't even be here."

"Sorry," Mabel whispered back. "I didn't mean to."

"No talking," Miss Reed barked, marching over and tapping Mabel lightly on the knuckles with her wand. Mabel winced. "Now, girls, I shall call out your names and you will step up to receive your broomstick and cat," Miss Reed said.

Winifred's name was called first, and Mabel tried to hide her disappointment as Winifred was given the cat she had been eyeing—a delicate creature with a glossy coat that trotted after Winifred, giving little jumps. By the time Miss Reed called Mabel's name, there weren't many cats left, and Mabel was handed a rather sleepy-looking, plump cat that refused to move, so she had to carry him back to her place. She hoped he would be better at flying than he was at walking.

"Now, watch carefully, girls, and I will demonstrate," Miss Reed said, holding her broom and sitting sideways on it. "Good posture is most important. Straight backs, please, as if you were doing the waft and glide." Winifred cut her eyes at Mabel and grinned, knowing how Mabel struggled with the waft and glide. "Make sure you slip your skirt loops over your shoes so your gown doesn't blow up when you fly." Miss Reed lifted the hem of her skirts to show off two foot-sized satin loops sewn on each side.

"I've been waiting and waiting to try my skirt loops," Winifred whispered, without getting told off by Miss Reed.

"Position your cat behind you," Miss Reed continued, "then in a clear, musical voice say, 'Avante!'" The girls watched as Miss Reed's broomstick took off and swooped sedately around the field, coming to land under the tree again. "Now, it's your turn, girls."

Ruby clung on to Mabel as she jammed her toes into the slippery loops. "I feel so unsteady, Mabel," she said, trying to balance on the broomstick. "This is hard enough. Why do we need to have the cats?"

"I think they act as a rudder," Mabel said. "Because your balance is uneven when you sit sideways. A cat makes it more stable, you see."

"Oh, help!" Ruby screamed, sliding backward off her broomstick. She landed on the grass with a thud.

"Ruby, are you all right?" Mabel knelt down beside her.

"Quickly, girls, back on, back on," Miss Reed ordered, clapping her hands.

"I banged my head," Ruby whimpered, struggling to sit up. Her eyes were watering.

As Mabel helped Ruby to her feet, she caught sight of

Miss Seymour's bicycle, propped up against the side of the broom shed. Why didn't they fly their broomsticks like that, instead of sitting on them sideways? It would be so much safer, Mabel thought, putting up her hand.

"Yes, Mabel Ratcliff, what is it?" Miss Reed said rather impatiently.

"I was just thinking," Mabel began, glancing over at Ruby and wondering if she should in fact say what she had been thinking, especially so soon after the liver fiasco. But it was such a good idea, and taking a deep breath, Mabel said, "I was just thinking that there might be a better way to fly on a broomstick. Without cats, I mean."

There was a rather long silence while Miss Reed stared at Mabel, her face getting redder and redder. "Excuse me?" she finally hissed. "Are you being rude deliberately?"

"No, no, I'm really not," Mabel replied. The rest of the girls had stopped practicing and were swiveling their heads between Mabel and Miss Reed.

With a furious scowl, Miss Reed said, "Witches have always flown with cats, Mabel Ratcliff. It's tradition."

"They haven't," Mabel whispered, glancing at Ruby, who was gingerly rubbing her head.

"You're going to get into trouble," Ruby mouthed.

"Well, they haven't," Mabel repeated, tears pricking

her eyes. Miss Reed was making her feel like she had done something wrong. But back in medieval times witches hadn't flown with cats. Witches hadn't flown sidesaddle either. They had learned that in history class last year. Sidesaddle wasn't introduced until the end of the fifteenth century.

"Mabel Ratcliff," Miss Reed boomed, puffing up like an angry bullfrog. "Just what are you suggesting? After your performance on Monday I'm surprised you even have the nerve to speak."

Mabel's mouth had gone dry, and her heart thundered in her chest. "Wouldn't it be safer to ride a broomstick like a bicycle?" she suggested, flinging one leg over her new broom to show what she meant. "You'd have much better balance this way and you wouldn't need the cat." Miss Reed's eyes had narrowed to tiny slits, and Mabel hurried on in a panic, desperate to make her teacher understand. "Shall I sh-show you?" Mabel stuttered, thinking that a quick demonstration might convince Miss Reed. Feeling too flustered to stop now, Mabel took off across the field. "See, you have so much more control like this," she called down, trying to gauge the look on Miss Reed's face. Mabel groaned in dismay as her dress blew up. She had forgotten to slip her feet back into her skirt loops. Still, at least Miss Reed could see how much sense it made to fly a broomstick this way. But the flying teacher didn't look convinced as Mabel landed on the grass. Her face was pulled into a sour twist, and trying another approach, Mabel said, "Think of all the money Ruthersfield would save on cream and fish for the cats." She smiled nervously, not sure what to do with her mouth.

A harsh thwack across her knuckles sent Mabel reeling into Ruby. "Wipe the smile off your face, girl, and go directly to Miss Brewer's office." She pointed her wand at Mabel's pinafore, and three more black *X*s joined the two she had received from Violet earlier in the week. "Such insolence is not to be tolerated," Miss Reed fumed.

Mabel could see Winifred smirking as she turned to go.

"I'll look after your cat for you," Ruby murmured. "You were only trying to help."

Mabel nodded gratefully, but as soon as she was away from the class, her eyes pooled with tears. She didn't deserve to be hit. Miss Reed was not being fair. Girls fell off their broomsticks all the time, and Mabel's idea was a good one. She trudged up the school steps, dragging her feet as she headed toward Miss Brewer's office. Again.

Chapter Nine

....

A Sewing Spell

MABEL RATCLIFF," MISS BREWER REMARKED, STARING AT Mabel out of eyes that still managed to intimidate, beneath their folds of droopy reptilian skin. "How nice to see you. Five demerits in three days, plus a suspension." The headmistress shook her head. "That is not what we expect from our girls."

"I'm really sorry, Miss Brewer." Mabel sniffed as she explained what had happened.

"Don't you have a handkerchief?" Miss Brewer inquired, and when Mabel shook her head, the headmistress handed her a clean, crisply pressed one from her desk drawer.

Mabel gave her nose a good blow. "I felt so bad for poor Ruby, and it just seems like a much safer way to fly," she finished up.

"Here at Ruthersfield, we pride ourselves on our traditions," Miss Brewer replied. "Riding a broomstick the way you suggested would be most inappropriate."

Mabel bit her lip. "But don't you think . . . ," she began, her words petering out as Miss Brewer raised an eyebrow. "I'm sorry, Miss Brewer," Mabel sighed. "I really didn't mean to be disrespectful."

Miss Brewer was silent for a while, proceeding to read a letter on her desk while Mabel stood in front of her, folding the handkerchief into a tight square. After about five minutes, the headmistress looked up and sighed. "You can go now, Mabel."

"But I haven't polished your crystal balls yet, Miss Brewer."

"Yes, you have, Mabel, rather recently if I recall. You will be better served by going to your sewing class."

"We're making flying cloaks," Ruby whispered, as Mabel slipped into her seat.

Miss Seymour beamed at the class. "In honor of your first flying lesson, we're going to be designing travel wear today." Her fat auburn ringlets bobbed around her ears like springs. "Who would like to demonstrate?" Winifred stuck her hand in the air, and Miss Seymour pointed her wand at her. "Come on up, Winifred."

Fluffing out her skirts, Winifred flounced to the front of the class. "Now, be as creative as you like," Miss Seymour said, "but remember, these cloaks have to be practical as well as attractive." Winifred chose a bolt of deep purple velvet from the fabric shelf and spread it over the worktable like Miss Seymour had shown them. "Now draw on your creative magic and picture the cloak in your head, Winifred. Just like you did when you made your spell apron." Winifred shut her eyes and concentrated. "Wait till you can feel your magic fizzing," Miss Seymour said. Winifred nodded. "Can you see the cloak clearly?" Miss Seymour asked.

"Oh, yes," Winifred sighed. "It's quite beautiful."

"Right then, whenever you're ready, Winifred. Say the design spell, and remember the upward flick of your wand at the end."

Taking a deep breath, Winifred waved her wand over the fabric and called out, "Creataclothis." A cloud of violet and blue smoke swirled around the fabric, and a whirring, snipping sound could be heard. When the smoke cleared, drifting in wisps across the sewing room, there, draped across the table, was a cloak. Miss Seymour held it up and the girls *oohed*.

"It's beautiful, Winifred," Florence Steiner said.

"Yes, simply stunning," Diana Mansfield agreed.

"Very nice," Miss Seymour said, turning the cloak around, "if a touch lopsided, Winifred. And perhaps a little much with the feathers?"

"A little much?" Ruby whispered to Mabel. "There must be at least a flock of peacocks stuck on there."

"I think it's perfect," Florence said with a simpering smile. "Well done, Winifred."

"Oh, yes, well done," Diana agreed.

"Who's next?" Miss Seymour mused, looking around the room. "Mabel Ratcliff, I think. Come along, Mabel. Let's see what you can do." Mabel got up and tramped to the head of the class. She picked out a bolt of brown woolen tweed.

"That's a nice practical color," Miss Seymour commented.

"So dull," Winifred murmured. "But practical," she added quickly, noticing Miss Seymour frowning at her.

"Now, picture just what you'd like to wear when flying," Miss Seymour said, turning her attention back to Mabel.

Mabel scrunched up her face and was silent for a few moments while she thought. "Creataclothis," she finally said, waving her wand in the air and remembering the little upward flick at the end. This time there was a cloud of brown and green tweedy-colored smoke swirling around the table and a sharp clipping sound from inside. When the smoke cleared, Miss Seymour held up Mabel's flying cloak. Except it wasn't a flying cloak at all. It was a pair of men's trousers. The class burst into raucous laughter, and Mabel blushed.

"I—I tried to focus on making a cloak, I really did, but my mind kept drifting to those," Mabel said, nodding at the trousers. She hung her head in shame. "Wouldn't it be more sensible to wear something like that when flying? Then we wouldn't have to worry about showing our petticoats," she mumbled, waiting to be sent right back to the headmistress's office.

Miss Seymour looked furious, and Mabel hunched her shoulders, preparing for the angry outburst that she knew was about to come.

"This whole class is showing great disrespect," Miss Seymour snapped. "You will all write out one hundred lines for me, saying, 'I shall treat my classmates as I would expect to be treated myself.'" Miss Seymour tossed her head, sending her curls spinning. She took some deep, calming breaths and turned Mabel's trousers around. "An unusual design, but these are exceptionally made, Mabel. Unfortunately you will not be able to wear them to school because they are not part of our uniform, but your hemming is even and the buttons on the pockets are attractive and practical at the same time."

"So your wand doesn't fall out?" Ruby suggested.

"Exactly, Ruby. Nice observation." Miss Seymour raised her chin a notch, and Mabel couldn't help feeling surprised. There was something bold and slightly defiant about the sewing teacher's response, as if by admiring Mabel's trousers she was exposing a side of herself that had been hidden before. Just like her bicycle-riding side, Mabel thought.

"But, Miss Seymour," Winifred remarked, glancing at Florence and Diana. "Those are most unfeminine and not the least bit attractive. Girls don't wear that sort of thing. Men do." Winifred gave a delicate shudder. "I would rather wear an old flour sack."

"Would you please leave the room, Winifred Delacy? I didn't ask for your opinion, and I'm sure Miss Brewer will have something to say about it."

Winifred opened her mouth to complain but thought better of it. She had never been sent to Miss Brewer's office before, and giving a sulky curtsy, she turned and left the classroom, throwing Mabel a look of fury on her way out.

For the first time since starting school, Mabel felt as if someone was taking her ideas seriously. That she wasn't completely insane to imagine trousers would be a much better thing to wear on a broomstick rather than layers of skirts and petticoats. And even though Miss Seymour hadn't come out and said it, Mabel was certain that the sewing teacher agreed with her.

"I'll do half your lines for you," Mabel offered, waiting in the lunch queue with Ruby and trying to avoid eye contact with Mrs. Bainbridge. "You didn't laugh at my trousers, Ruby, so you shouldn't have to do the punishment."

"Thanks." Ruby smiled. "And I thought your trousers were extremely original."

"You should be doing my lines," Winifred said, turning around and glaring at Mabel. "Since it's your fault we got them in the first place."

"I'll help you, Winifred," Florence offered.

"So will I," Diana quickly agreed. "I'm sure your father will be terribly upset."

"I'm sure he'll complain to Miss Brewer when he hears how I've been treated," Winifred said. She looked down her nose at Mabel. "Miss Brewer should have expelled you, Mabel Ratcliff. I had a stomachache for hours after eating your liver. Why Ruthersfield accepted you in the first place is a mystery. You don't know the first thing about being a witch." She gave a disgusted sniff. "You can't dance the waft and glide. You slouch over a crystal ball. And you have no sense of style. Witches do not wear trousers. Nor do ladies."

"My mother says a lady shouldn't say spiteful things either," Ruby said quietly.

"What does your mother know about ladies?" Winifred scoffed. "She's just a canal worker's wife."

A deep red flush spread up Ruby's neck, and she flinched at Winifred's words.

"You're so cruel, Winifred," Mabel burst out. "That's such a mean thing to say. Why do you always have to be so horrible?"

For a moment Winifred looked taken aback. She wasn't used to girls standing up to her, and Mabel felt suddenly nervous, unsure what Winifred might do. Florence and Diana glanced at each other uneasily, and Winifred's face hardened. "You better watch it, Mabel Ratcliff." Turning away, she slipped her arms possessively through Diana's and Florence's. "Come on, girls. I've lost my appetite. Mabel's probably poisoned the sausages."

"Thank you for defending me," Ruby said after they had left. "Winifred seemed really mad, didn't she?"

"Yes, she did," Mabel agreed, "and I probably shouldn't have said what I said. But I don't regret it. Winifred is mean."

Ruby gave her a warm smile. "You're a good friend, Mabel."

"That's nice to know," Mabel joked rather shakily. "Because with Winifred against me, I need all the friends I can get." Out of all the girls in the school, she had definitely picked the worst one to make an enemy.

······································

Chapter Ten

A Cottage by the Canal

AFTER COLLECTING THEIR BROOMSTICKS AT THE END of the day, Mabel and Ruby watched Miss Seymour wheel her bicycle out of the broom shed. Miss Reed stood nearby with her arms folded, a look of utter disgust on her face.

"I don't think our flying teacher approves," Ruby murmured. "She looks furious."

"Gosh, I think that's the most wonderful thing I've ever seen," Mabel said. "Can I touch it, Miss Seymour?" she called out.

"Be my guest," Miss Seymour replied. "I'm still rather wobbly when I ride, but it's great fun."

"Are you going to come to school on it every day?" Mabel asked, running her hands over the smooth, black, metal frame.

Miss Seymour laughed. "Gosh, no! I only rode here the past few days because poor Bramble has been suffering with an infected paw. He's going around limping and refuses to get on my broomstick. And I can't fly without a cat, of course."

Mabel ran her fingers over the shiny metal spokes, touching the chain and the pedals, examining how it was made, and imagining a bicycle that could be ridden across the sky.

After a few minutes Ruby cleared her throat. "Mabel, I think Miss Seymour wants to go," she said.

"Gosh, I'm sorry." Mabel jumped up. "It's just so magnificent."

"Could we move along, please?" Miss Reed called out, sounding annoyed. "There are girls waiting to take off. You're creating a holdup." She waved her arms in furious circles, directing broomstick traffic around them.

"Time to go," Miss Seymour said, and climbing onto her bicycle, she pedaled madly toward the school gates, ringing her bell to clear a pathway.

"First day flying home without a chaperone," Mabel said, patting the back of her broomstick. "Come on,

Lightning." She hoped the name she had chosen for her cat might give him a little more zip. Not that she expected him to prance about like Violet Featherstone's cat did. It would just be nice if he moved at something faster than a lazy waddle. Reluctantly he got up off the ground and flopped down behind Mabel.

"There goes Winifred," Ruby sighed, as Winifred wobbled past them, her cat perched gracefully behind her. She didn't look down, but Mabel could see the expression of smug satisfaction on her face. "I just can't seem to get my balance," Ruby said, rising a few feet off the ground. "It's sitting sideways like this. I keep thinking I'm going to slip off again." She brushed a sleeve over her eyes, and Mabel realized she was crying.

"Do you want me to fly home with you?" Mabel suggested, knowing this might make her late, but hating to see her friend so upset. "I don't have to," she added quickly, not wanting to make Ruby uncomfortable. The girls had been friends for four years now, and although Ruby had been over to Mabel's house for tea a few times, she had never invited Mabel back. Not that Mabel minded, because Ruby didn't invite anyone over, saying her house was too small and crowded.

Ruby hesitated a moment and then nodded. "I won't be so frightened of falling if I know you're beside me."

"We can't fly more than six feet off the ground for the first week anyway," Mabel reminded her. "So if you do fall, it won't be far."

With a great deal of shakiness, Ruby and Mabel turned left down Glover Lane, Mabel's broomstick dipping at the back because of Lightning's extra weight. "It's hard to fly level," Mabel panted. "And my feet keep slipping out of these skirt loops."

"I know. Mine too. You should have worn your trousers, Mabel."

"Can you imagine Miss Brewer's face if I did!"

"Hey, look out," a gentleman shouted, as Mabel zigzagged overhead, knocking off his top hat with her shoe. "You beginners are a hazard to pedestrians."

"Sorry, sir," Mabel called back. This was so different from the floating she had done as a child. There was nothing airy or free-form about it. You had to concentrate, and Mabel guessed that their backs would be stiff and achy in the morning from holding themselves so straight.

"Thanks for flying with me," Ruby panted, heading up toward Canal Street. The road veered off down a grassy track, and Ruby hovered a second, as if she were making up her mind about something. "Would you like to come in for tea?" she finally said. "It's not a big house, and it doesn't have fancy things in it like yours, and I've got lots of sisters, and it can get noisy and—"

"I'd love to," Mabel interrupted, beaming at her friend. "I'd just love to." Nanny Grimshaw would be cross, but it was worth getting punished for, Mabel decided. If she missed this opportunity, Ruby might not ask her again. And with a sense of recklessness, Mabel followed Ruby down the track that led toward the canal. Two horses clopped along the bank, pulling a barge slowly behind. The barge blew its horn at them, and Ruby gave an embarrassed smile.

"That's my pa," she said, lifting one hand quickly off her broomstick to wave at a man on the boat deck wearing a white shirt with the sleeves rolled up and a cloth cap. "He's taking a shipment of stone down to London."

"Hello, Mr. Tanner," Mabel called out. "Nice to meet you." Ruby's dad put his fingers in his mouth and whistled at the girls, a loud, sharp whistle that Mabel found most impressive. She decided that if she got to know Mr. Tanner a little better, she would ask him to show her how it was done.

"Here we are," Ruby huffed, landing in front of a tiny cottage that sat beside the canal. It was set back from the water a little ways, with a stone wall surrounding the property. "It's not very fancy," Ruby apologized, as a woman came out of the cottage. She had a white cotton scarf tied around her head and four little girls hanging from her skirts. They all had the same fine, butter-colored hair and pale blue eyes as Ruby. As soon as the children saw Ruby's cat, they pounced on him with squeals of delight and carried him inside the cottage.

"And who is this?" the woman said, pressing a hand against the small of her back and giving Mabel a tired smile.

"This is Mabel, Ma. She flew home with me because I was a bit scared to try it by myself." Ruby fiddled with her shirt collar "I asked her to stay for tea."

"Pleased to meet you, mam," Mabel said with a curtsy.

"Well then, you'd better come in," Mrs. Tanner said, and before Mabel could finish replying, Ruby's mother had hustled her inside the cottage and Mabel found herself sitting at a table, crowded with all Ruby's sisters, eating a piece of caraway cake.

Seeing Mabel trying to count heads, Ruby said, "There's eight of us in all. Not counting Ma and Pa of course."

"All girls," Mrs. Tanner sighed, looking around the table. "But I wouldn't trade a one of them."

"Where does everyone sleep?" Mabel asked,

realizing right away that this was a rude question and none of her business.

"Ma and Pa have one room with the two little ones," Ruby said. "And the rest of us share the other. Three to a bed." Mabel tried not to show her surprise.

"Yes, and Ruby is the worst kicker," one of the oldest girls remarked. "She's always knocking me onto the floor."

"Ruby's the worst kicker and Ruby's the only witch," a little girl cried out, banging her tin mug on the table. "Ruby's a witch, Ruby's a witch," she chanted.

"That's enough, Camellia." Mrs. Tanner put a finger against her lips.

"Camellia! What a beautiful name," Mabel burst out. "I love flower names. I wish I'd been called Magnolia," she added wistfully.

"Oh, I think Mabel suits you," Mrs. Tanner said, which was not what Mabel wanted to hear. "Anyway, it took us quite off guard when we found out our Ruby had the gift. I still haven't recovered from the shock," she remarked, unable to hide her pride. "None of us have. The only witch we know of in the family is Ruby's great-aunt Ethel. She was a tea leaf reader in a carnival."

"This was her ring," Ruby said shyly, showing Mabel a thin silver band that she wore on her thumb.

It had a green stone in the center carved into the shape of a sickle moon. "I never take it off," Ruby added. "It makes me feel connected to her."

"Ruby's learning magic like Great-Aunt Ethel did," another little girl said. "She can do spells. Can you do spells?"

"A few," Mabel replied, feeling a little overwhelmed by the small space and all these sisters. "This is a delicious cake," she said, finishing the last crumb on her plate.

"Ma's a wonderful baker," Ruby pronounced. "You'll have to come back and try her plum tarts."

"Not that I can promise this lot will leave you any," Mrs. Tanner said affectionately. She rubbed at her swollen knuckles. "So are you familiar with any of the witches in your family, Mabel? What they did? Where they lived?"

"I—I'm not sure," Mabel said, realizing she knew nothing about her magical past. It would be nice to have a ring like Ruby's though. Something from one of her witch ancestors that she could wear and show the girls at school.

"I hope you didn't mind my mother asking all those questions," Ruby said, walking Mabel outside after tea. "She's just excited to meet another witch, that's all. It's such a novelty in our family, you see."

"I think it's a bit of a novelty in my family too," Mabel admitted. There were no books on the subject in their house. No portraits or photographs of famous witch relatives hanging on display, or magical mementos passed down through the generations. And for the first time in her life, Mabel realized just how odd this was.

....

Chapter Eleven

Daisy's Hair Problem

MABEL'S CAT HAD FALLEN ASLEEP IN MRS. TANNER'S chicken coop, snuggled up in one of the nesting boxes. It was Ruby who found him. She hauled him out by his tail. "Come on, you lazybones. This is not your house." Lightning waddled toward Mabel's broomstick and heaved himself on board. He yawned and licked his whiskers, as if he'd just done an extremely hard day's work. Stroking his back, Mabel could feel him purring beneath her hand.

"See you at school tomorrow," Ruby said, waving to Mabel. "And thank you for flying me home." She paused a moment, then burst out, "I'm sorry you got suspended, Mabel, I really am. It's a stupid rule of Miss Brewer's, not letting you experiment."

"Ruby!" Mabel laughed. "You said 'stupid.' I've never heard you say that word before."

"Well, it is stupid," Ruby said stubbornly. "You have the best ideas, Mabel. Miss Seymour thinks so too. You could tell she liked your trousers."

"Thanks." Mabel wiggled her feet into her skirt loops. She was beginning to feel extremely nervous about facing Nanny Grimshaw. What had she been thinking? Going to another girl's house without permission, especially since that girl was Ruby. Mabel could tell Nanny Grimshaw disapproved of the Tanners by the way her mouth tightened whenever Mabel mentioned them. The only girl she might not have minded Mabel spontaneously having tea with was Winifred. According to Nanny Grimshaw, a lord's daughter would be a much more fitting companion than a canal worker's. Not that Mabel regretted having tea at Ruby's. But the thought of Nanny with her pinched face, tapping her umbrella on the floor when she found out, was enough to make Mabel groan out loud. She'd never be allowed to fly without a chaperone again.

"Are you all right, Mabel?" Ruby asked in concern. "You look rather ill."

"I just need to get home," Mabel said. Pointing her broomstick skyward, she called out, "Avante," and flew shakily into the air.

Her palms were damp, and Mabel kept tipping back and forth, trying to find her balance. Lightning started meowing, and Mabel got more and more anxious as she flew. Nanny Grimshaw would send her to bed with no supper. She'd never let her see Ruby again. Mabel was wobbling up Trotting Hill, flying about four feet off the ground, when the Trimbles' dog, Jeeves, shot out of their gate and came bounding toward her. Mabel squealed and slid backward, landing in a heap on the road.

"I'm so sorry," Mrs. Trimble cried out, racing after Jeeves, who was licking Mabel all over her face. "Are you hurt?"

"I don't think so." Mabel pushed Jeeves away and straightened her glasses. She got up gingerly, brushing her skirt. Lightning was standing with his fur all ruffled, hissing at Jeeves.

"Are you quite sure you're all right?" Mrs. Trimble asked, wringing her hands.

Mabel nodded, her eyes welling up. Now Nanny Grimshaw would be even more cross, because her clothes were dirty. Picking up her broomstick, Mabel started to run, Lightning waddling along after her.

Mabel's lip wobbled as she stumbled around the side of the house. If she had to face Nanny Grimshaw, she would do it from behind Daisy's skirts. With a deep, shaky breath, she pushed open the back door and burst into the kitchen.

"What in heavens?" Daisy said, putting down her rolling pin. She dusted her floury hands on her apron and opened her arms wide. Mabel hurtled into them, smelling apple pie, and the tears that had been building up inside her came flooding out.

"I'm so sorry I'm late, Daisy. I had tea at Ruby's and then I fell off my broomstick. Is Nanny Grimshaw f-furious?"

"Calm down," Daisy murmured, rubbing Mabel's back.

"I can't calm down. She won't let me play with Ruby again, or have any supper."

"Miss Mabel," Daisy raised her voice, "Nanny Grimshaw's upstairs with one of her headaches."

"What?" Mabel sniffed, pulling away. She looked up at Daisy in disbelief. "She's in bed?"

"Has been for the past two hours. Said I was to make sure you didn't have more than one bun for tea and that you worked on your embroidery afterward."

"Really?" Mabel started to smile. Relief flooded through her. She took her glasses off and wiped her eyes. "I was so scared, Daisy. I thought she'd be waiting for me with her umbrella."

"Well, you shouldn't have gone off without telling us," Daisy said sternly, handing Mabel her handkerchief. "That was naughty. You're lucky your mama is at one of her rose growers' meetings, otherwise you'd be having her to deal with too."

"I am sorry, Daisy. But Mama would understand. She likes Ruby. And Ruby never asks anyone in for tea, so I had to say yes. And I only flew home with her because she was scared of riding her broomstick." Mabel took a deep breath and blew her nose. "We have to fly sidesaddle, which is why I fell off. I'd never have fallen if I'd been allowed to ride my broomstick like a bicycle." Mabel started to cry again, more from relief this time. "It has not been a good day."

"Sit down and I'll get you a nice mug of cocoa," Daisy said.

"Can I stay in the kitchen with you, Daisy? Please?" Mabel begged. "I don't want to go up to the nursery by myself."

"If you sit quietly and don't get in my way. No fiddling with things."

Mabel settled herself in the chair by the fireplace. She picked up yesterday's newspaper from the top of a stack of papers that Daisy kept to start the fire with. "Suffragettes petition to give women the right to vote," Mabel read, studying the headlines. "What's a suffragette, Daisy?"

"I said sit quietly, not pester me with questions." Daisy shook her head. "Suffragettes believe women should be able to vote too. Not just men. They want equal rights."

"Are you a suffragette, Daisy?"

"I don't have time to be a suffragette," Daisy said, pouring milk into a pan.

"It says they've been collecting signatures in favor of women voting and they're going to give their petition to the prime minister."

"Good luck with that," Daisy muttered. "He'll never do anything."

"But if enough people sign it, won't he have to listen?" Mabel asked, staring at the paper. "Maybe I should start a petition, saying we should all be allowed to fly our broomsticks the way you'd ride a bicycle. The girls would love that. We wouldn't be worried about falling off all the time. Poor Ruby is terrified of broomstick flying. Lots of girls are."

"Now, don't go getting into any more trouble, Miss Mabel."

"But, Daisy, it would be so much safer. And so much more fun," Mabel couldn't help adding. "I could get all the students to sign it, and then I'd give it to Miss Brewer."

Daisy rolled her eyes, spooning cocoa powder into a mug. "I'm quite sure your headmistress wouldn't approve."

"I bet Miss Seymour would. I bet she'd think it was a great idea. It can't hurt to try," Mabel said. "And I wouldn't be breaking any rules. I'll be right back, Daisy."

Mabel tiptoed into the drawing room and took a sheet of pale blue writing paper out of her mother's desk. Then, listening for sounds from upstairs, she hurried back into the kitchen. Using a corner of the table that didn't have flour on it, Mabel wrote across the top of the paper in her best handwriting: "All Ruthersfield girls should be able to sit astride their broomsticks instead of riding them sidesaddle. The use of cats should be discontinued." She thought for a moment before adding, "And girls should have the right to wear trousers when flying." Underneath Mabel signed her name.

As she looked around for Daisy to see if she would sign too, a loud shriek came from the pantry. Mabel leaped up and dashed across the kitchen, to find Daisy standing in the pantry doorway, hands on her hips. She was glaring at Lightning, who had settled himself on one of the shelves next to the cream bowl and was calmly licking his paws.

"That creature snuck in here and ate all my cream," Daisy fumed. "I don't know where he came from, but I want him out of here. Now."

"That's Lightning," Mabel said, feeling rather relieved he'd followed her home. She'd forgotten all about him after her fall. "He's my flying companion. He's very friendly," she said. Giving Daisy an apologetic look, Mabel added, "I'm afraid he's going to be living with us from now on."

"Is that necessary?" Daisy grumbled. "I would really rather he didn't."

"If I get enough signatures on my petition, he won't have to," Mabel replied, hoping this might calm Daisy down. "We'll be able to ride our broomsticks without cats."

"Well, put my name at the top of the list," Daisy said. "Pesky beast!" With an indignant yowl, Lightning leaped off the shelf and landed on poor Daisy's shoulders. She screamed and bent over, giving a violent shake. Her cap fell off, but Lightning clung on, pawing at Daisy's bun. "Scat!" Daisy screeched, jiggling frantically. There was a flurry of black fur and Lightning dropped to the floor. Picking him up, Daisy marched right over to the back door and tossed the cat outside.

"Daisy, I think he caught a vole," Mabel called out, staring at the furry thing lying beside Daisy's cap. She crouched down and gave it a poke. "No, it's too big to be a vole. And it's all curled up and a lovely glossy brown."

"Give that back, Miss Mabel," Daisy cried, rushing into the pantry. "It's mine." She grabbed the furry thing off the floor, two pink spots of color staining her cheeks.

"Your hair!" Mabel gasped in shock, noticing that the thick, soft bun that normally peeked out from beneath Daisy's cap was no longer on her head. It was, Mabel realized, clutched in Daisy's hands. And even though she knew it was extremely rude, she couldn't stop staring as Daisy reached up behind her and pinned the bun back into place, running a hand over the thin, wispy hair that covered the rest of her head.

"I had no idea," Mabel blurted out. "That's not your real hair?"

"No, it's not," Daisy snapped, pulling her cap back on. "And the show's over, so you can stop gawking." Glancing away, she said, "I'd appreciate you keeping this to yourself, Miss Mabel. It's embarrassing enough, wearing a hairpiece without the whole world knowing."

"Of course, Daisy. I'm so sorry," Mabel said, not sure what she was apologizing for but hating to see Daisy so distressed. "I won't say a word to anyone, I promise."

"It's vain, I know, caring so much about my looks. Always hiding my hair under a cap. But it's so thin, constantly splitting and breaking, and it never seems to grow." Daisy sighed. "I've always wanted to look like Nellie Glitters, with her long auburn locks, all glossy and thick. Not this thin, brittle stuff I've been cursed with." She tossed her head, as if she were tossing an imaginary curtain of hair. "I even bought some of that Mr. Pinkham's hair tonic you see advertised in the newspaper," Daisy admitted. She gave a disgusted sniff. "It promised me thicker, longer hair in two weeks, but nothing happened, apart from my wasting two shillings."

"I'm so sorry," Mabel said again, handing Daisy back her handkerchief.

"I'm scared it's going to get thinner and thinner. What if I start to get bald patches?" Daisy blew her nose. "If that happens, I'm never leaving the house."

Mabel nibbled a piece of roast chicken from the carcass on the shelf beside her. "A hair-growing potion," she whispered, finding it difficult to ignore the fizzy feeling bubbling inside her. "That's what you want, isn't it, Daisy?"

"Is there such a thing?" Daisy asked, looking uncomfortable and slightly wary. Picking up a jar of sugar, she turned and walked back into the kitchen.

"I don't know," Mabel said, following along behind.

"You don't know?" Daisy watched Mabel open her satchel and rummage through it. "You mean you're going to experiment, don't you?" She pressed her knuckles against her hips. "After what happened on Monday?" Daisy shook her head and snorted. "Miss Brewer will expel you if she finds out."

"Ruby says I have great ideas," Mabel said, pulling a copy of *Traditional Magic: A Study Guide for the Student Witch* out of her satchel. "And Miss Brewer will never know. This has nothing to do with school, Daisy. I just want to help you." Mabel looked up at Daisy, and with a great deal of passion said, "No one should have to wear a hairpiece."

"You know all the right things to say, don't you?" Daisy muttered, starting to line a pie tin with pastry.

"There's a simple growing powder in here. We're making it in class tomorrow. It's meant to be used in gardens, but hair is a bit like a plant, don't you think? It has roots and it grows."

"That's stretching it a bit," Daisy said, chopping apples into the tin.

Mabel chewed at her lip. "Perhaps I'll add a pinch of Icelandic dwarf beard for thickness and curl," she murmured softly.

"Dwarf beard! No thank you."

"But it's lovely, Daisy. We mixed some with lamb's wool in knitting class last term, and it made the most wonderful fuzzy shawl, so thick and soft it was like wearing a cloud. Oh, and maybe a spoonful of dried phoenix flames for color? The powder is a deep, dark red," Mabel explained. "Just like Nellie Glitters's hair. We use it to dye blankets because the color never fades. It's also supposed to put the warmth back in a cold marriage," she whispered. "But only the teachers are allowed to make that potion."

"Sounds like a lot of nonsense," Daisy muttered, but she was stroking her neck and sighing, as if imagining what a mane of beautiful curls might feel like.

"Please let me try. We could test a bit of your hair first, and if it doesn't work out, I can fiddle about with some different ingredients and try to invent something that does."

"Fiddle about?" Daisy raised her eyebrows. "See, you do like to fiddle."

"Come on, Daisy. Just think how happy you'd be if you looked like Nellie Glitters."

"That may be, but I'm not sure I want you using magic on my hair."

"Please," Mabel begged. "I really believe I can help you."

Daisy sprinkled sugar over the apples and grated

on a little nutmeg. "I'll consider it," she said at last, touching a hand to the back of her head.

Mabel gave what she hoped was a confident smile. She didn't have any idea whether she could turn Daisy's hair into a long, thick, auburn mane, but she was dying to have a go.

Chapter Twelve

....

Secrets

NANNY GRIMSHAW APPEARED IN THE KITCHEN JUST AS Daisy was putting her pie in the oven. "I expected to find you in the nursery," she said, staring down her long nose at Mabel. "Working on your embroidery." Nanny Grimshaw had decided that Mabel should make a tablecloth, which required endless flowers being embroidered all over it.

"I—I was studying in here," Mabel said, holding up *Traditional Magic*. "After flying right home from school," she added, noticing Daisy roll her eyes. "How's your head, Nanny?" Mabel asked, hoping to distract her from noticing the broomstick petition, which was lying out in full view on the table.

"My head is bearable," Nanny Grimshaw replied, walking across the room.

Mabel sprung out of her chair. "Shall we go up to the nursery now, then?"

"And what might this be?" Nanny Grimshaw remarked, reaching out a bony hand and plucking up the sheet of blue paper.

"It's nothing," Mabel said, throwing Daisy a panicked look.

"Nothing?" Nanny Grimshaw held the paper close to her eyes and studied it. Then in one swift movement she crumpled the petition into a ball, dropped it on the floor, and stepped on it.

"That was mine," Mabel said, wishing she could turn Nanny into a frog.

"And where might you be getting such ideas from? I'm sure your mother would be horrified if she knew you were stirring up trouble, trying to get the girls to sign a petition." Catching sight of the *Gazette*, Nanny Grimshaw stalked over to the chair. She peered down at the headlines. "This is precisely why little girls should not be reading the newspaper," she said. "It gives them ideas above their station."

"Custard or cream with the pie?" Daisy asked, trying to lighten the atmosphere.

"Mabel will not be having dessert tonight," Nanny Grimshaw said. "Until she apologizes for such defiant behavior." Nanny Grimshaw gave one of her sniffs. "It's a good thing I stopped such nonsense before you took that petition to school, otherwise you'd find yourself in a great deal more trouble." She stared at Mabel, waiting for her to apologize. But Mabel couldn't say it. She wasn't sorry. Nanny Grimshaw tapped her shoe. "I'm waiting."

Mabel shook her head, watching Nanny Grimshaw's face turn the color of an overripe plum.

"Upstairs to bed." Nanny Grimshaw pointed at the door. "Insolent child."

As Mabel shuffled across the room, she decided that a frog was too nice for Nanny Grimshaw. She should be turned into a beetle, and then Mabel could step on her.

"I couldn't smuggle you up any pie," Daisy whispered, slipping into Mabel's room half an hour later. "Nanny's watching me like a hawk. But I did want you to have this," Daisy said, taking Mabel's petition from her pocket. "It's still a bit crumpled, but I put the iron on the stove and pressed it for you best I could."

"Oh, Daisy, thank you." Mabel flung her arms around the maid.

"I might not have time for this suffragette business, but I know a good idea when I see one. I've signed my name, see, right under yours." Daisy lowered her voice. "Just keep it hidden from old Grimface, otherwise we'll both be in trouble."

It was starting to get dark, and Mabel lay in bed wishing that her mother would come home. To stop herself from feeling sad she concentrated on possible ideas for hair potions. If Icelandic dwarf beard didn't work, she could try dandelion fluff for softness. There were all sorts of interesting possibilities, and Mabel was still coming up with ideas when she heard the front door open. A few minutes later Nora walked into the room, smelling of rose water and fresh air.

"Mama," Mabel cried out. "I'm so pleased you're home."

"I heard all about it from Nanny." Nora sighed, sinking down on the edge of the bed. "She is feeling most upset."

"Nanny's so mean," Mabel whispered, sitting up. "She hates me."

"Now, Mabel, Nanny Grimshaw doesn't hate you. Quite the opposite, in fact. She worries about you, darling. You have to understand that Nanny is rather old-fashioned. She's just trying to protect you, that's all. She doesn't want to see you get into trouble."

"Mama, I don't think I need a nanny anymore," Mabel said. "I'm at school all day, and Daisy can help me with getting up and bedtime."

Nora laughed. "And what about weekends, and when I'm out at my meetings? I had my nanny until I was sixteen." She patted Mabel's hand. "Let's remember this is Nanny's home too. She's been with us for eight years. And I'm quite sure there's a kind heart under all that frostiness." Mabel didn't say anything. She just picked at a thread on her quilt. It was impossible to explain how awful Nanny Grimshaw was to her, because she behaved so differently around her mother.

"So I'm guessing your first flying lesson wasn't as fun as you expected?" Nora said, smoothing the collar of Mabel's nightgown.

"It's dangerous, and uncomfortable, Mama. Most of the girls hate it. I've already had a fall. So has Ruby. She was really scared. That's why I flew home with her."

"You flew home with Ruby?" Nora said. "Does Nanny know?"

"No, she was sleeping off one of her headaches. And I shouldn't have done it without asking, but Ruby was too frightened to fly by herself, and then her mother asked me to stay for tea, and . . ."

"You had tea at Ruby's? Good gracious. I did miss all the excitement."

"You mustn't tell Nanny though. Promise me, Mama. I won't do it again."

"No, you won't. Not without asking."

"She has seven sisters," Mabel continued, "and their cottage is tiny. Her mother made a caraway cake. I didn't see much of her father. He was on one of the canal boats, but I'm going to ask him if he'll teach me how to whistle."

"Goodness." Nora smiled.

"Mrs. Tanner was telling me about Ruby's great-aunt Ethel. She was a witch in a carnival." Mabel could see the light from her candle flickering against the wall. "So I was wondering about the witches in our family," she said softly. "Maybe there are pictures or photographs somewhere. Or stories you can tell me?"

Nora cleared her throat, but she didn't speak.

"The girls at school talk about their roots all the time," Mabel said. "We all know Winifred Delacy's great-great-grandmother was a crystal ball gazer to the king of England. And her aunt is a famous palm reader living in Paris. She can go right back to the twelfth century." Mabel rubbed at the lace on her sleeve. "It would just be nice to have a ring or something, like Ruby has from her great-aunt Ethel. Something to show the other girls, so I can have a story of my own to share."

"Well, now, I'm not quite sure," Nora said, glancing down at her hands. "I have never really explored our magical roots." They sat in silence for a few moments, and then, getting to her feet, Nora picked up the candle. "Time for bed," she said rather briskly. In the silvery light, Mabel could see the same closed expression her mother always wore whenever Mabel brought up the past.

Walking across the room, Nora stopped halfway and turned around. "You mean the world to me, Mabel," she said softly, as if this explained everything.

After Nora had gone, Mabel lay alone in the dark, wondering what sort of secrets her mother was keeping. And why she didn't trust Mabel enough to share them.

Chapter Thirteen

....

The Petition

"RISE AND SHINE," NANNY GRIMSHAW CROWED, FLINGING open Mabel's curtains.

Mabel dragged herself out of bed and splashed cold water on her face from the big china bowl in the corner. This was meant to stimulate blood circulation, according to Nanny. Still yawning, Mabel struggled into her uniform. Then Nanny Grimshaw brushed her hair, giving it one hundred firm strokes before plaiting it into two tight braids and tying the ends with purple ribbon.

"Where is Mabel's porridge from yesterday?" Nanny Grimshaw inquired, eying the plate of fresh baked scones on the table. "I seem to remember she didn't finish it."

"I'm afraid Mabel's cat ate it," Daisy said sweetly, putting a scone on Nora's breakfast tray next to the teapot and newspaper.

"Indeed." Nanny's lips tightened, clearly not believing a word. "Just one then," she said. "No need to be greedy, Mabel. And I'd like a kipper, Daisy."

Mabel shot Daisy a grateful look. "I'll be right back," Daisy muttered, trotting toward the pantry. Mabel could feel Lightning's soft body pressed up against her legs. Glancing under the table, she saw a fat kipper tucked between his paws. Not wanting to be around when Daisy discovered the theft, Mabel slipped her satchel over her shoulder and bent down. She hefted Lightning into her arms and kicked the kipper away.

"You're a naughty boy," Mabel whispered, as Lightning gazed at her out of big green eyes. He rubbed the side of his head against Mabel's pinafore, giving a deep rumbling purr.

"Straight home after school, Mabel," Nanny Grimshaw ordered. "We will be working on your tablecloth."

"Yes, Nanny," Mabel said, staggering across the room. She grabbed her broomstick from the umbrella stand and was nudging open the back door with her foot, when Daisy let out one of her impressive screams.

"That beast has stolen a kipper," Daisy yelled. Mabel let the door slam shut behind her, plunking Lightning on the broomstick and taking off as fast as she could manage, which wasn't very fast considering she had to sit sideways.

"You are a useless, furry lump," Mabel muttered, but there was a whisper of affection in her voice as she flew down Trotting Hill.

The second Mabel landed, Lightning waddled inside the academy with all the other cats, searching for a sunny corner, while Mabel stood outside with her petition, shuffling her feet and feeling too scared to approach anyone.

"Can I help you, Mabel?" Miss Seymour said, walking over. She made a slowing motion with her hands as Emily Bisset in year nine swooped by, slipping off her broomstick as she landed. Emily stood up to show she wasn't hurt, and Miss Seymour gave an irritated shake of her head. "Far too fast." She peered at Mabel. "Are you feeling all right, Mabel? You look like you've forgotten where to go."

"No, I'm fine, thank you," Mabel replied. But as Miss Seymour walked off, she hurried after her. "Actually, Miss Seymour, can I show you something?" Mabel's legs had gone shaky, and she was breathing fast as she held out her piece of paper. "It's a petition," Mabel said, her heart speeding up as Miss Seymour started to read. "Ruby and I both fell off our broomsticks yesterday," Mabel explained, nervously filling the silence. "Ruby hurt her head. That's why I'm trying to get signatures."

Miss Seymour smiled. "Did I give you this idea, Mabel? About riding a broomstick like a bicycle?"

"Actually you did," Mabel admitted. "It's just that I think we would have a lot more control sitting astride than sitting sideways."

"I agree," Miss Seymour said, reaching into her bag and pulling out a pen.

"You do?" Mabel couldn't hide her surprise. She watched Miss Seymour hold the paper in one hand and sign her name under Daisy's.

"There was a rather controversial article in last week's *Magic Cauldron* about the dangers of flying sidesaddle," Miss Seymour said, surprising Mabel yet again. "I'm not sure how well received it was, but it got me thinking."

Mabel still hadn't recovered from the shock as she stood by the gates, trying to persuade a few of the girls to sign.

"I don't want to get in trouble," Beth Harper apologized. "We heard how angry Miss Reed was with you yesterday, and I couldn't bear to get my knuckles whacked."

Martha Davenport told Mabel that she wished she could sign, but if Miss Brewer saw her name on the list, she might tell her parents, and they most certainly wouldn't approve.

"My papa thinks that we shouldn't ride broomsticks at all," Helen Juniper sighed. "He says as the weaker sex we don't have the strength for it, and he's already worried I might faint in the air."

"I don't think we're the weaker sex," Mabel said, thinking of Daisy lugging in buckets of coal for the fire, or beating all the rugs in the house to get the dust out.

By the end of the afternoon Mabel had managed to acquire seven more signatures to add to her petition. There had been a fair amount of positive interest, but only Ruby, Tabitha, four girls in year five, and Miss Seymour had had the courage to sign. Winifred had laughed in Mabel's face when she heard what Mabel was trying to do.

"That is the most undignified idea I've ever heard of. No lady would dream of riding any way but sidesaddle. You're going to get yourself expelled if you're not careful." Winifred patted her ringlets and put her hat on, tipping it sideways at a jaunty angle. "My papa doesn't approve of rebel witches. He says a rebel witch is just as bad as an evil witch and should be locked up in prison."

"I am not a rebel," Mabel said hotly.

"You just don't want to admit it's a good idea," Ruby broke in, "because Mabel thought of it and not you."

Winifred turned away and linked her arm through Florence's. "It's a terrible idea, and we have to go," she said, smirking at Mabel. "You won't believe what my papa is picking us up in—his motor car! We're the only people in the country who have one. He had it shipped all the way over from France and it arrived today!" With their cats following behind them, Winifred and Florence wafted out of the main building and glided elegantly down the stairs.

"Come on." Mabel grabbed Ruby's arm. "I've read about motor cars in the paper. They're like a carriage you steer without horses." The girls raced after Florence and Winifred, just in time to see them climbing into a shiny black motor vehicle. Lord Winthrop Delacy sat in the front wearing a leather driving hat and goggles.

"Oh, that's a beauty," Mabel sighed, watching as the car roared out of the gates. "It's the most amazing invention, Ruby. They don't need to be fed like horses, or get tired, and can go twice as fast as a carriage."

"Impressive, isn't it?" Miss Seymour said, standing

nearby. "I believe that in a few years' time everyone will be driving those or riding bicycles."

"What rot." Miss Reed snorted. "A horse or broomstick is far more reliable. I certainly wouldn't trust riding in one of those machines."

"It's going to be a new century soon," Miss Seymour said. "Things are changing."

"Not for the better," Miss Reed snapped, and swirling around, she marched back up the steps.

"Change is never easy," Miss Seymour remarked, smiling at Mabel and Ruby. "It scares people."

"I know," Mabel agreed. "I only got seven signatures for my petition today."

"Well, don't give up," Miss Seymour said, pulling on a pair of purple flying gloves. "Good ideas are worth pursuing, Mabel."

....

Chapter Fourteen

Mabel Experiments— Again

AS MABEL FLEW HOME (LEAVING RUBY WOBBLING HER way along Canal Street) she thought about the little vial of growing powder she had managed to slip into her pinafore during enchanted gardens class. They had sprinkled some onto a clump of rather tired-looking morning glories that were now climbing their way merrily up a trellis behind the school. "This will help keep your gardens vibrant and alive," Miss Spooner had said. "And every lady needs a beautiful garden to entertain in."

"Well, every lady needs a full head of hair too," Mabel whispered to Lightning, as if this could justify her experimenting again. But hadn't Miss Seymour just said that good ideas were worth pursuing? And this, Mabel felt sure, was an excellent idea. She shivered with anticipation, thinking about the little clump of dwarf beard nestled in her satchel, alongside the twist of brown paper holding a spoonful of dried phoenix flames. She had dashed into the spell room after lunch and gathered what she needed while Miss Mantel was still finishing up her jam roly-poly and custard.

With an undignified bump, Mabel landed in the front garden. She hurried around to the back of the cottage, hoping to catch Daisy alone in the kitchen. As she passed by the greenhouse, she could see her mother inside, scoring the stem of a rosebush with a knife. Looking up, Nora smiled and waved, and Mabel opened the greenhouse door.

"What are you doing, Mama?" she asked, watching Nora bind a small cutting from another plant onto the stem of the bush she had just slashed.

"I'm hoping to graft these two varieties together," Nora said. "Would you like to stay and assist?"

"I'm afraid I can't. I'm helping Daisy with something," Mabel replied, glad for once that her mother was so busy. Now all she had to do was stay out of Nanny's way so she could mix up the hair potion. Unfortunately, this was not as easy as Mabel had hoped, and slipping into the kitchen, she stifled a loud groan. Standing there, with her arms folded, shoulders jutting out like vulture wings, was Nanny Grimshaw. She gave Mabel a sour smile. "A proper lady always uses the front door, Mabel." Nanny must have been watching from the window, Mabel decided, waiting to pounce as soon as she walked in.

After Mabel had eaten a piece of plain bread and butter, Nanny marched her straight upstairs to the nursery, where she now sat, embroidering a rose onto her tablecloth. Mabel stared at the pink lumpy blob, wondering how many more of these things she was going to have to embroider. "Until it is covered," Nanny Grimshaw had said crisply when Mabel got up the courage to ask. "Now, enough of your chatter," she said, and popped a mint into her mouth.

Sometime later, glancing at the clock on the mantelpiece, Mabel realized that she had been embroidering for over an hour. "Could I take a little break, Nanny?" she asked. There was a crick in her neck and her thumb was sore and tingly from getting poked. Nanny Grimshaw didn't reply, and looking over, Mabel noticed that Nanny's head had nodded forward and a soft snoring was coming from the direction of her chair. Without hesitating, Mabel stood up and crept across the room. This was extremely risky, but she didn't need long. As soon as she was out of the nursery, Mabel raced downstairs to the kitchen.

"Where's Nanny?" Daisy said, turning around from the stove.

"She's asleep, Daisy, so we have to hurry."

"Hurry?" Daisy gripped her wooden spoon.

"To mix up your hair potion," Mabel whispered. She took the bottle of growing powder out of her pinafore, scattering white dust over the floor. "Oh, it's leaked." Mabel grimaced, wiping her hands down her skirt. "This stuff is everywhere." Hurrying across to the fireplace, she held open her pocket and brushed the spilled powder into the grate. A clump of something sticky was stuck to the inside fabric, and pulling it free, Mabel realized it was her cobweb experiment. "Interesting," she murmured, shaking off the powder and dropping it right back in her pocket.

"You're making a huge mess," Daisy muttered, and then rather more anxiously, "And do we have to do this now?"

"I'm just going to dilute the growing powder," Mabel said, walking to the sink and dripping some water from the tap into the bottle. The liquid turned misty, and she rushed back to the table, digging the tuft of dwarf beard out of her satchel. She dropped in a few soft hairs, and immediately the potion bubbled up, little woolly clouds puffing into the air. Whenever one popped, it sounded like somebody sneezing.

"What on earth . . ." Daisy gasped, as Mabel opened the twist of paper and sprinkled a pinch of dried phoenix flame into the bottle. The liquid started fizzing, and they watched it turn a deep, rich red.

"Ohhh, that's beautiful," Mabel whispered. "Isn't it the most lovely color?"

"Just like Nellie Glitters's hair," Daisy sighed, staring dreamily at the bottle. Getting a grip on her senses, she added, "But I am not, under any circumstances, putting that anywhere near my hair. How do I know it won't all fall out?"

"Oh, I really don't imagine that's likely," Mabel said, trying to control her excitement. She didn't want to scare Daisy off. "I've worked with these ingredients before." Which happened to be true. She had just never mixed them all together. "And think how wonderful it would be if you didn't have to wear the—"

"All right, all right," Daisy snapped. "You don't have to say that word out loud."

"Just rinse the potion in before bed, and tomorrow, when you wake up, you should have long, soft, red curls like Nellie Glitters's."

"Ummm." Daisy chewed on her lip.

"If you're nervous, Daisy, you could test a bit of your

hair first," Mabel suggested, feeling just the tiniest bit anxious herself. It made sense in her head, blending these ingredients together, but with no one to ask, she couldn't help thinking about the liver disaster.

"Ummm," Daisy said again, eyeing the bottle of potion. "I'll consider it, Miss Mabel. Now, get yourself back upstairs before Nanny Grimface wakes."

"Daisy, do you think we could petition to get rid of Nanny?" Mabel proposed. "I'll write one out, and if we both sign it, Mama would have to consider letting her go."

"Don't I wish," Daisy muttered. "Honestly, I'd keep that kipper-stealing cat of yours over old sour face any day."

Nanny Grimshaw was still snoring away in her armchair when Mabel crept back into the nursery, and by the time she opened her eyes, Mabel was hard at work on her embroidery. The rest of the evening passed uneventfully enough, except for Lightning helping himself to a lamb chop. Mabel had no idea whether Daisy planned to use her hair potion or not. But she had a strong suspicion that the answer was probably yes when a sharp, high-pitched scream woke her the following morning.

Leaping out of bed, Mabel raced across the landing. "Please don't let Mama and Nanny wake up," she prayed, flinging open the door to Daisy's room and giving a rather loud shriek herself. "Daisy?" Mabel gasped, staring at the cloud of bright pink hair puffing upward from Daisy's head. It had grown at least two feet, but in the wrong direction, and looked rather like an enormous, fluffy candle flame. Curls of pink smoke drifted around it, and reaching out a hand to touch, Mabel was shocked by how warm and soft it felt.

"My hair!" Daisy wailed, turning from her mirror. "What have you done?"

There was a long moment of silence. "I'm so sorry, Daisy. I thought you were going to just test a bit," Mabel whispered at last, wondering what on earth had gone wrong.

"Easier said than done," Daisy hissed. She glared at Mabel. "It kept dribbling over my scalp, and I decided it would be better to have all my hair look the same. Big mistake that was."

"Well, it's certainly grown. And it is lovely and soft."

"It looks like the cotton candy they sell at the circus," Daisy rasped. "I could be part of a freak show."

"It would make a wonderful hand-warmer," Mabel suggested, thinking this was rather a good idea. "Tuck your hands inside on cold days," she added, lifting her arms above her head to demonstrate in case Daisy didn't understand what she meant.

Daisy grabbed a magazine from her dressing table and held up the picture of a beautiful young woman with long, auburn curls. "I look nothing like Nellie Glitters," she sobbed. "Nothing at all."

Mabel had to agree. "You don't, but we're not going to give up, Daisy. I'll keep working on this, I promise."

"No, you won't," Daisy snapped, surprising Mabel with her sharpness. She shook her head vigorously and her puffy pink hair swayed back and forth. "What was I thinking?"

"Will you tell my mother?" Mabel asked, dreading to think what Nora would say.

"I should," Daisy grunted, narrowing her eyes. "But the truth is I'm too embarrassed to show this to anybody."

"Would you like me to cut it off for you?" Mabel whispered. "It won't take long for your old hair to grow back in. And you can cover it with your cap, Daisy. No one will be able to tell." There was a rather strange smell of burning feathers in the room, which Mabel had only just noticed.

"No, thank you very much," Daisy said. She glanced back at the mirror and shuddered. "I've well and truly had it with your experimenting."

....

Chapter Fifteen

The Society of Forward-Thinking Witches

Have you noticed that Miss Seymour and Miss Brewer seem to be spending an awful lot of time together lately?" Ruby remarked one morning. The girls were on their way to potions class when Miss Seymour swept out of the headmistress's office and hurried off down the corridor. "I'd love to know what's going on. Whatever it is, it's making Miss Brewer all grumpy," Ruby said. "She snapped at me yesterday for having wrinkles in my stockings. But Miss Seymour's been going around beaming. Mabel? Are you listening?"

"Sorry. It's just so hot," Mabel sighed, wanting to peel off her damp, itchy petticoats. "And my neck aches from practicing swan posture in palm reading. All that sitting still and looking elegant is exhausting." And pointless, Mabel thought in dejection. It had been two weeks since her suspension, and after Daisy's refusal to let Mabel near her hair again, a flat heaviness had settled inside her. As if nothing really mattered very much. She had even stopped trying to collect signatures for her petition. "Perhaps it's the weather that's making Miss Brewer irritable," Mabel suggested. "Nanny's certainly been worse than usual."

A lot of the cats seemed troubled by the heat too, hissing and scratching and refusing to get on their broomsticks.

"Which is why," Miss Mantel told the girls in potions class, "we will be making a cat-calming brew. Witches' cats are high-strung creatures and rather sensitive to the heat."

"Yes, they are," Tabitha agreed. "Carbonel nipped me this morning, and kept arching his back when I was flying. I almost fell off."

"Well, this works like a charm," Miss Mantel said. "You'll have your kitty eating out of your hand in no time. It's a nice, simple recipe, just evening dew and catnip."

"I wish it worked on nannies too," Mabel muttered, opening *Traditional Magic*. "'A way to make your kitty more pleasant,'" she read. "'If your cat is prone to biting and hissing, this potion will calm him down, turn him into a gentle flying companion.'" Mabel stared at the page. Nanny wasn't a cat, but maybe a little calming potion would make her more pleasant? Perhaps she'd even let Mabel play outside for a change.

"Why are you taking that with you?" Ruby asked, as Mabel slid a bottle of cat brew into her satchel at the end of class. "Lightning is a sweetheart. He doesn't need calming down."

"No, but Nanny Grimshaw does," Mabel whispered. "I probably won't use it," she added, seeing Ruby's anxious face. "It's just nice to have on hand. And it's only catnip and evening dew. It can't hurt her."

"You are completely out of your mind, Mabel."

"You would be too if you had to live with my nanny," Mabel said, dragging along the corridor toward sewing class.

Miss Seymour seemed in an exceptionally good mood. Her eyes sparkled as she greeted the girls. "Before we start work on our sweet dream pillows, I have a few announcements. First, make sure your hands are dry before handling the phoenix feathers. They stick terribly to sweaty palms. Second"—Miss Seymour looked around the class—"we have an important guest visiting from London tomorrow, so please be on time. Some of you in particular, I think, will be most fascinated to hear what she has to say." She was smiling at Mabel as she spoke, and for the first time in a long while, Mabel's toes started to tingle. A soft breeze blew through the open window, stirring the heavy air and bringing with it a waft of possibility.

With all Mabel's good intentions of getting to school early the next day, she ended up being fifteen minutes late. Nanny had insisted on porridge for breakfast, and Mabel gulped down as much as she could manage before pushing her bowl away.

"Tomorrow's breakfast," Nanny said, taking the bowl through to the pantry. "I'm putting it on a high shelf," she called out, "so that cat can't get it." As Mabel tried to leave, Nanny Grimshaw had marched her back upstairs for a clean handkerchief, and then again to change her stockings, which had a tiny hole in the left leg.

By the time Mabel tiptoed into the great hall and slipped into the seat Ruby had been saving for her, the whole school was already assembled. "Mabel, where were you?" Ruby whispered.

"Couldn't get away from mean, old Nanny," Mabel panted. "She will definitely be getting some cat-calming brew tonight. Has anyone noticed I'm late?"

"No. The teachers are all in a flap over this special visitor. I do know it's a witch," Ruby whispered, "because she has a broomstick parked outside with letters carved on it. *SOFTW*—whatever that means."

"I think we're about to find out," Mabel murmured, as Miss Brewer walked onto the stage, accompanied by Miss Seymour and a tall witch in black robes, with bangs of frizzy red hair showing from under her hat.

"Silence," Miss Brewer barked, although there was no need for such a statement because the girls had already quieted down. "I have always believed in the sort of magical education we offer our students here at Ruthersfield," Miss Brewer began. She glanced over at Miss Seymour and her jaw tightened. "But it has been brought to my attention recently that as we move toward a new century, it is time for us to re-examine the place witchcraft will take in this changing world." Mabel felt a thrill of anticipation race through her. She didn't know what was coming, but words like "change" and "re-examine" were full of promise. "So would you please give a warm welcome to Miss Angelina Tate, who is here to talk about the possibility, and I do stress *possibility*," Miss Brewer said, staring straight at Mabel, "of introducing a science program into our school curriculum."

Mabel clapped as hard as she could. "This is so

exciting, Ruby. And what a beautiful name Miss Tate has. Angelina," Mabel murmured, running the syllables over her tongue. "That is almost as lovely as Magnolia."

Winifred turned around. "You haven't even heard what she has to say yet, Mabel." The way Winifred pronounced "Mabel" made it sound even uglier and plainer than usual. "And why would a witch want to learn science anyway?" Winifred fanned herself with her hand. "It is so hot in here I feel quite faint." Leaning toward Florence, she whispered, "I wouldn't wish that color hair on anyone. It's as orange as carrots."

"Keep quiet, Winifred, and stop being mean," Mabel hissed, as the orange-haired lady began to speak.

"It is a great honor to visit with you here today. I am a Ruthersfield alumna myself." There was another round of clapping, and Angelina Tate held up her hand. "This is the age of science, girls. All around us new inventions are being created. The world is changing fast, and it is important for magic to change along with it."

"Oh, yes!" Mabel breathed, grabbing Ruby's arm.

"Until recently we have relied on the same spells that our ancestors used. Traditional spells passed down from generation to generation that will always have a place in society. But now is the time to dare to push boundaries and fly against the wind. To experiment with our magic and see where such new thinking leads us." Miss Tate paused a moment before saying, "So with the help of Miss Seymour, the Society of Forward-Thinking Witches is going to sponsor a competition here at Ruthersfield."

"A competition," Mabel whispered in excitement.

"If I may interrupt one moment," Miss Brewer said, stamping her cane for silence. "Any girl who chooses to enter will follow strict competition guidelines." Once again Miss Brewer's eyes were on Mabel. "Miss Tate has written a simple guide to spell construction with basic templates you can follow. There is a dictionary of ingredients in the back, and she has listed combinations of things that do and do not work well together."

"Chocolate liver!" someone whispered, setting off a ripple of laughter.

"We want you girls to come up with your own inventions," Miss Tate continued. "A new spell that will make the running of a household a little easier."

"Perhaps you could give the girls some examples?" Miss Seymour broke in.

"Of course." Angelina Tate smiled. "We just ran this competition at L'École Sorcellerie, the renowned school of witchcraft in Paris. The students entered some wonderful inventions—magic slippers that run errands for you, a cake that bakes without an oven

while you sing to it, buttons that do up by themselves."
Miss Seymour started clapping, and the girls followed
her lead, until Miss Tate held up her hand again. "Most
important of all, we want you girls to use your minds,
get your hands dirty. Embrace the world of science."

"I'm not getting my hands dirty," Winifred said. "I
always wear gloves when I mix up my spells. And why
would we want to create new spells?" she said, sounding
anxious. "The ones we have are perfectly good."

"Won't your father expect you to enter, Winifred,"
Florence said, "being on the board of governors?"

"I'm sure he will," Winifred sighed, wrapping a hair
ribbon round her finger.

"My papa will certainly complain to Miss Brewer,"
Florence whispered. "He thinks we're far too modern
here at Ruthersfield as it is. If he had his way, I'd be
home embroidering samplers with Mother all day long."

"I think it's wonderful," Ruby said. "Don't you,
Mabel?"

"I do," Mabel agreed, waving her hand in the air.

"Why do you always have to be so keen, Mabel?"
Winifred muttered.

Miss Brewer peered in Mabel's direction. "What a
surprise. You have a question, Mabel Ratcliff?"

The hall had gone quiet, and Mabel gulped down
her nerves. "I—I just wondered," Mabel began, wiping

her sweaty hands on her pinafore. "I wondered why our inventions had to be only for the household? Could we invent other things too, Miss Tate?"

"Such as?" Miss Tate said, stepping to the front of the stage.

"Well, I'd love to invent a broomstick that would fly to the moon," Mabel began, startled at the laughter that broke out. "Or shrinking buildings that fit in your pocket so you could move them wherever you wanted." As she sat down quickly, Mabel's chair scraped along the floor.

"Interesting ideas," Miss Tate said, "but right now those areas of science are not ones that women have much experience with. Hopefully in the future this will change."

Mabel wished she hadn't said anything, because Winifred was whispering in Florence's ear, and Florence was bent over, giggling behind her hands.

For the rest of day, every time Winifred walked past Mabel, she made a whooshing noise, sending Diana and Florence into spasms of laughter. When the last bell rang at the end of embroidery class, Mabel's curiosity finally got the better of her, and she asked the girls what was so funny.

"That's the noise my invisible broomstick makes when it flies to the moon," Winifred said, causing

Diana and Florence to collapse into fresh giggles.

"Ignore them," Ruby said, pulling Mabel into the corridor before she could retaliate. "You can't risk getting sent to Miss Brewer's office again. Winifred's just being mean because she knows you're going to invent something better than she is."

The girls were hunting for their cats in the great hall when Miss Seymour swept by. She stopped in front of them for a moment. "I loved what you said to Miss Tate this morning, Mabel. It's good to have dreams to follow. Don't lose that passion."

Mabel looked surprised. She blinked at Miss Seymour from behind her thick lenses. "I won't, I promise. And I'm so excited by the competition, Miss Seymour."

"I'm sure you are, but don't get too carried away, Mabel. Overambitiousness is what gets you into trouble. There's nothing wrong with a simple invention. You've got plenty of time to construct that rocket broomstick!" With a warm smile at the girls, she flew on.

"You're Miss Seymour's special pet, aren't you, Mabel?" Winifred said smoothly, stepping out of the shadows.

"Oh, keep quiet," Mabel muttered, resisting the urge to give Winifred a hard push.

"Well, we all know Winifred won't be entering the

competition," Ruby said. "She doesn't like to get her hands dirty."

"No, I have far more important things to concern myself with. Like a new dress fitting for a beautiful pale blue satin gown Mama has ordered for me." Winifred gave her curls a toss. "We're having a house party this weekend, and I'm going to be allowed to stay up for the dance." She practiced batting her eyelashes. "Mama says I can tell fortunes if I wish. We have some special houseguests coming to stay. Lord and Lady Gofry from Fandlemarsh and some old friends of Mama's from Melton Bay."

"How thrilling," Mabel said, noticing the way her skin always started itching whenever Melton Bay was mentioned.

Chapter Sixteen

....

A Much Nicer Nanny!

THE WHOLE WAY HOME MABEL THOUGHT ABOUT
inventions. If thin, slow-growing hair was something
a lot of woman suffered from and didn't talk about, then
maybe a magic hair potion would be a great invention
to enter in the competition, assuming she could make
it work. And assuming she could convince Daisy to let
her experiment again. It wasn't exactly a household
gadget, but it would certainly make a lady's life much
pleasanter. The instant Miss Seymour had handed out
the spell construction guides, Mabel had looked up
dried phoenix flames in the index. She was fascinated
(and a little horrified) to discover that when mixed

with a cold ingredient, like a blast of north wind, polar bear breath, or *Icelandic dwarf beard*, the color changed and the heat source was activated. Which was why, Mabel realized, Daisy's hair had been so warm. And pink! And all that hot air had made it puff up. Well, at least now she knew, although it would have been nice to have such information before she began experimenting.

As soon as Mabel got home that afternoon, she raced to the greenhouse, but her mother wasn't there. Mabel found her in the drawing room, scribbling notes and reading about cross-pollination. "Mama, there's a competition at school," she burst out. "We get to make our own inventions, and I have to tell you all about it!"

"My goodness! That does sound exciting." Nora closed her book and smiled. "Then we must have tea together."

"Really, Mama?" Mabel could hear Nanny's shoes clomping down the stairs. "You won't change your mind? You promise."

Nanny Grimshaw appeared in the doorway. "Hello, Nanny," Nora said. "Are you looking for Mabel?"

"Indeed I am," Nanny replied with a brisk smile. "Come along, Mabel. You shouldn't be disturbing your mother like this."

"Oh, she's not disturbing me one bit," Nora said. "We're about to have tea."

"But, mam, Mabel has her embroidery to do, and a pair of stockings to darn."

"That can all wait," Nora said, much to Mabel's relief. "Why don't you have a nice cup of tea in the kitchen with Daisy and a read of the newspaper, Nanny?"

"I don't approve of newspapers," Nanny said tartly. "And I will take my tea in the garden." With a sharp nod at Nora, she stalked out of the room.

"I'll tell Daisy," Mabel offered, wanting an excuse to go to the kitchen.

"Good thing I made a seedcake," Daisy said when she heard, dabbing a handkerchief over her cheeks. Beads of sweat glistened on her flushed skin, and she looked awfully hot beneath her bonnet. It was an old wool one that covered her whole head, but ever since the hair disaster Daisy had refused to take it off.

"You're the best, Daisy," Mabel said, giving her a hug.

"Sucking up to me doesn't mean I've completely forgiven you, Miss Mabel," Daisy remarked rather tartly. And Mabel decided that perhaps this was not the best time to suggest trying out another hair experiment.

"Mama says we can have our tea in the drawing room," Mabel said, tipping a couple of drops of cat-calming potion into the single cup on the small tray. "This is going out to Nanny, isn't it?" she asked, as

Daisy placed a milk jug and a slice of cake on the tray.

"Why are you so interested?" Daisy said suspiciously.

"I just want to make sure Nanny enjoys her tea, that's all."

Over cucumber sandwiches and seedcake, Mabel told her mother all about the Society of Forward-Thinking Witches and the competition they were organizing through the school. "Can you believe it, Mama? We're going to start learning about science." Mabel swung her feet in excitement. "Why spells work and what happens when you mix different ingredients together. About time too," Mabel added. "I can't wait to come up with an invention of my own. Finally, I can start experimenting without getting into trouble."

"Well, thank goodness for the Society of Forward-Thinking Witches," Nora said, clinking her teacup against Mabel's.

Mabel gave a little shiver. "I was thinking about making a pair of magic hands, Mama. You're always saying you could do with an extra set while you work."

"I certainly could," Nora said. "But how would you manage such a thing?"

"I don't know," Mabel confessed. "I just like the idea." She was just helping herself to a third slice of cake (making the most of Nanny's absence) when the drawing room door burst open.

"I think you better come quickly, mam," Daisy said, speaking to Nora but staring at Mabel. "Nanny's acting very strange."

"What seems to be the matter?" Nora got to her feet.

"You'll see, soon enough."

Nanny Grimshaw was lying on the lawn in a patch of sun. She had her arms and legs stretched out to the sides and her face turned upward.

"Nanny!" Nora said. "Whatever are you doing?"

"Meow! I'm sorry, mam." Nanny struggled to her feet. "It just looked so nice and sunny over there."

"Nanny, are you feeling all right?" Nora asked, while Mabel tried to avoid her mother's gaze.

"I feel all warm and fuzzy inside," Nanny said, nuzzling her head against Nora's arm.

"Are you purring, Nanny?" Nora said in alarm. "It sounds as if you're purring." Nanny Grimshaw started walking around her in circles, rubbing her head all over Nora.

"Nanny, stop it." Nora tried to step away. "I think you should go and lie down. Should I call the doctor?"

"I don't believe there's any need for that, mam. She'll be better when she's had a little sleep. You can help me take her up," Daisy said, eying Mabel sharply.

Nanny Grimshaw kept stopping to rub against the banisters as they shepherded her upstairs. Mabel could still hear her purring. When they finally got her onto her bed, Nanny Grimshaw smiled up at them and gave a sleepy meow.

"I don't know what you've done, Miss Mabel, but she better be back to normal in the morning," Daisy murmured.

"Come on, Daisy. You can't pretend you don't like her like this. She's so much pleasanter. I even feel quite fond of her," Mabel said, stroking Nanny Grimshaw on the back. "Who's a nice nanny then?"

They left her purring away under the covers, and Mabel had a wonderful evening. She got to eat as many sausages as she wanted, and Nora even read her a bedtime story.

When Nanny Grimshaw came down for breakfast the next day, she gave Mabel a hard, suspicious look. "It appears I was unwell yesterday. Not at all myself."

"Well, you seem nicely rested now," Daisy interjected, handing her a cup of tea.

"This has something to do with you, Mabel Ratcliff, I just know it does," Nanny hissed, "and I intend to find out what."

Too nervous to finish her last bite of scone, Mabel excused herself from the table.

"How did it go?" Ruby asked when Mabel got to school. She was rubbing at a fresh bruise on her chin. "With your nanny, I mean?"

Ignoring the question, Mabel peered at Ruby's face. "Where did that come from?"

"I fell," Ruby admitted. "I don't want to talk about it though." She rubbed her eyes. "I just hate flying a broomstick."

"I'm going to work on getting more signatures for my petition," Mabel said, feeling a renewed sense of energy. "Then I can take it along to Miss Brewer next week."

"Tell me about your nanny," Ruby asked again. "What happened?"

"Nanny Grimshaw made a really nice cat, but I think she got suspicious when she started purring."

"Just concentrate on the competition," Ruby begged. "You're only going to get yourself in trouble."

This was good advice, and throughout the weekend, Mabel came up with all sorts of different ideas. She considered inventing special shoes for Daisy with springs in them so with one big leap she could be home from the shops. Or a teakettle that called out to you when it was boiling, so even if Daisy was in the garden, she'd hear it screaming, "I'm boiling, I'm boiling." Or how about dishes that leaped in the sink and washed themselves?

By Monday morning, Mabel couldn't wait to share her ideas with Ruby. She was also determined to try to gather a few more signatures for her petition. As soon as Mabel got to school, she positioned herself by the academy gates, waving her petition at the girls as they trailed in. "Please sign," Mabel begged. "Riding sidesaddle with a cat is dangerous and outdated. We've got to change the rules." She managed to secure five more signatures and quite a lot of interest, especially from the younger girls.

"Mabel, you are being ridiculous," Violet Feather-stone said, swooping past her with her chaperone group. "Miss Brewer will never allow us to ride the way you are suggesting. It's a shocking thing to propose."

"But why is riding with the broomstick between your legs shocking?" Mabel said, watching Violet's cheeks turn pink. "It's sensible. In medieval times witches used to perform in circuses. They would do dives and spirals, and all sorts of acrobatics on their broomsticks."

"Thank goodness those days are past," Violet said. "That is not how a lady behaves."

"I think we should start up broomstick sports," Mabel suggested, at which point Violet pulled out her smelling salts and stiffly marched her chaperone group into school.

Winifred breezed past with Florence and Diana. She gave Mabel a curious look, then leaned over and whispered something to Florence. Every few steps the girls kept glancing back, but Mabel did her best to ignore them. She watched Miss Reed and Miss Seymour land on the pavement and, carrying their broomsticks, they walked toward her, cats trotting behind.

"This is nonsense," Miss Reed said, frowning at Mabel. "I'm surprised Miss Brewer hasn't put a stop to it. Causing trouble, that's what this is. And riding bicycles to school doesn't help matters," she muttered under her breath.

Ignoring Miss Reed's comment, Miss Seymour said, "Have you taken your petition to Miss Brewer yet, Mabel?"

"I'm a little scared of what she might say," Mabel admitted. "But I will."

Miss Seymour turned to Miss Reed. "We've had five girls end up with concussions this year because of slipping off broomsticks. I think it's time the school addressed this issue."

"Girls fall off broomsticks because they don't pay attention," Miss Reed snapped. "Not because they ride sidesaddle." She stalked off toward the broomstick shed, and Mabel hoped she wasn't going to report her to the headmistress.

"I plan to talk to Miss Brewer about this matter myself," Miss Seymour told Mabel. "Would you like me to come with you when you drop off the petition?"

"I'm going to do it now, before history," Mabel said. "Before I lose my courage."

"Then I will have to wish you luck, because I'm on corridor duty, but I can walk inside with you if you like?" Miss Seymour accompanied Mabel as far as the great hall. "Girls, no running in the corridor," she called out as a group of year-three students raced past. "You know the rules." Turning back to Mabel, Miss Seymour gave her an encouraging smile. "You'll be fine, Mabel. Just be yourself."

It took all Mabel's courage to knock on the headmistress's door.

"Come in," Miss Brewer called out, raising her eyebrows when she saw Mabel enter. "Shouldn't you be on your way to class?"

Remembering to curtsy, Mabel stuttered, "I . . . umm . . ."

"Well, don't hum and ha, girl. What are you here for?"

Mabel's hands were all sweaty as she put the petition down on Miss Brewer's desk. She could see that the ink had smudged in places. "Some of us feel . . . ," Mabel began.

"Speak up, Mabel Ratcliff. I can't hear you."

Raising her voice, Mabel said, "Some of us feel that riding broomsticks sidesaddle is dangerous." Miss Brewer frowned and picked up the petition. With a loud swallow, Mabel continued. "Ruby Tanner has fallen off six times. She's lucky not to have broken any bones. We should ride them like bicycles, Miss Brewer. It would give us much more control, and we wouldn't need the cats. The cats are only there for balance," Mabel said, glancing at the headmistress.

Miss Brewer didn't respond. Her face was stony as she studied the petition. "There are fourteen names on here, Mabel."

"But a lot of the girls are interested, Miss Brewer. They were too scared to sign," Mabel added.

"Indeed." Miss Brewer pursed her mouth. She dropped the petition on her desk and stared straight at Mabel. "You may go now."

"Might you think about it?" Mabel asked bravely. "Please, Miss Brewer?"

"There is nothing to think about, Mabel. We are dealing with enough change in this school as it is."

"Yes, Miss Brewer," Mabel sighed, and dropping a curtsy, she turned to leave.

Chapter Seventeen

....

Winifred Causes Trouble

"HOW DID IT GO?" RUBY ASKED AS THEY WALKED DOWN the corridor to their history of magic class.

"Not well," Mabel replied, staring at the floor. "Not well at all."

"I'm so sorry, Mabel." Ruby touched her on the arm.

Mabel looked up and nodded, pushing her glasses into place. She found herself staring at the back of Winifred Delacy's golden head. Winifred was walking in front with a group of girls clustered around her.

"And my gown was stunning," Winifred said. "Everyone remarked on it."

"She's talking about the big house party her family

had this weekend," Ruby whispered. "Just wait. I bet she says what a brilliant witch everyone thought she was."

"Of course, my father had made a corner of the ballroom into my fortune-telling salon," Winifred continued. "I wore a real gold tiara, and my crystal ball gazing was so admired, Lord Stratton said he would certainly be telling Queen Victoria."

"Oh my!" Ruby whispered, opening the door of the history room. "Queen Victoria!" She pretended to wave smelling salts in front of her face, making Mabel smile. "I shall faint from the shock!"

History of magic was one of Mabel's favorite subjects. They had just finished learning about the great rebel witch Annabelle Lewis, who had defeated an evil uprising in 1592, and Mabel decided that Annabelle Lewis was her new favorite heroine. As well as having a beautiful name, Annabelle had flown around the country, trying to gather support, and had been the first witch to stand up to the grand high priestess when it was discovered she was practicing black magic. There had been a song written about her, which they had learned in music class, and Mabel had gone around humming it for weeks.

"Good morning," said Miss Harcourt, their history teacher, as the girls sat down at their desks. "Today we are going to be studying our own personal histories. Each girl will make a family tree, highlighting her magical roots."

"Oh, how marvelous," Winifred said, and then in a lower voice to Florence, she whispered, "This should be fun!"

"But first, let us share some of our memorable witch ancestors with the class," Miss Harcourt said.

Mabel felt as if her stomach were full of moths. She glanced around the room, seeing if any of the other girls looked troubled by this. None of them did. In fact, as far as Mabel could tell, they all seemed delighted by Miss Harcourt's announcement.

Winifred immediately put her hand up. "My great-great-grandmother was a crystal ball gazer for the king of England," she said. "I have one of her original crystal balls. And my aunt is a witch. She lives in Paris. We have strong magical roots, Miss Harcourt."

"Thank you, Winifred. That is most interesting. Would anyone else like to share?"

Ruby put her hand up. "My great-aunt Ethel was a tea leaf reader in a carnival, Miss Harcourt." Mabel saw Winifred and Florence exchange grins. "As far as we know she was the first witch in our family," Ruby added, rubbing her thumb ring. "My parents were really proud when I got the gift."

"I'm sure they were, Ruby." Miss Harcourt smiled at Ruby and then turned to Mabel. "And how about you, Mabel Ratcliff?"

Mabel flushed. She didn't want to be the only one who knew nothing about her ancestors.

"Mabel?" Miss Harcourt prompted. "I'm asking you a question."

"I . . . ," Mabel began. She gave a soft sigh. "I don't know of any witches in my family, Miss Harcourt." Tabitha gave her a sympathetic look.

Winifred put her hand up again. "Miss Harcourt," she said, glancing at Diana. "It's not really fair asking Mabel about her magical roots when she doesn't know who her parents are." There was a gasp from the class, and Winifred blurted out, "It can't be easy being found in a flowerpot."

Mabel blinked behind her glasses. There was a fuzzy ringing in her ears, and she gripped the edge of her desk, feeling like she couldn't breathe in enough air. All the girls were staring at her, even Ruby.

"There may be evil magic in Mabel's past, for all we know," Winifred continued. "That could be the reason Mabel was abandoned."

"That is not true," Mabel burst out, finding her voice at last. "You are lying, Winifred. I hate you." Mabel pushed back her chair and stood up.

The girls gasped again, more loudly, and Winifred stood up too. For a moment she looked frightened, as if she knew she had gone too far. "How dare you accuse me of lying, Mabel Ratcliff. My words are the absolute truth. Miss Eliza Cranford, one of our houseguests this weekend, informed us of your situation."

"You liar," Mabel shouted, lurching at Winifred.

Miss Harcourt pulled her wand out of the knitted case hanging from a ribbon around her waist and pointed it at the floor. A cloud of purple smoke shot out with a loud bang. "That is quite enough," Miss Harcourt snapped. "I will not tolerate this behavior in my classroom."

Mabel shoved Winifred hard in the stomach. "I hate you," she croaked, her voice thick with tears. Turning, Mabel ran from the room. She bolted along the corridor and down the stairs, clattering across the great hall.

"Mabel Ratcliff, where are you going?" Violet Featherstone called out. Mabel ignored her and pushed open the front doors. She blinked against the sharp sunlight, blinded for a moment after the gloom of the academy. Stumbling down the wide stone steps, Mabel started to run. She ran as hard as she could, trying to get away from the memory that had surfaced in her head, the memory of a beach on a hot summer day, and Eliza Cranford's cruel words. "Your mother was an earthworm. She lived in a flowerpot." That was what Eliza had said, and Mabel cried as she ran down Glover Lane, suddenly understanding what Nora had been hiding from her all these years. Mabel wasn't her child.

"Why didn't you tell me?" Mabel sobbed, pushing past Nanny Grimshaw and into the drawing room, where she found Nora at her desk. "You're not my real mother, are you?"

Nora flinched and put down her pen. "Mabel, what are you saying?" she gasped. "Where did you get such information?"

"Eliza Cranford," Mabel cried out. "She was the girl who used to tease me back in Melton Bay. And now I know why. Because you found me in a flowerpot!"

"You will not speak to your mother in that way," Nanny Grimshaw fumed, following Mabel into the room.

"Mabel, please," Nora said, hurrying over.

"Is it true?" Mabel sobbed. "Have you been pretending all this time to be my mother? Was I abandoned as a baby?"

"Mabel." Nora's face drained of color. She held out her hand. "It's not like that."

"And Dr. Ratcliff. He's not my father, is he? Is he?" Mabel repeated. Nora slowly shook her head. "You should have told me," Mabel cried out. "And to hear it from horrible Winifred Delacy."

"Oh, Mabel, please," Nora said, but Mabel was already squeezing past Nanny, trying to get to the stairs.

"Not so fast," Nanny Grimshaw exploded, grabbing Mabel by the arm. "You insolent, rude child. I have never seen such disrespectful behavior. Talking back to your mother, screaming." She pulled Mabel into the hallway and yanked her umbrella out of the stand. "Hold out your hand," Nanny Grimshaw ordered, raising the umbrella above her head. "This deserves a proper beating."

"No," Nora shouted from the doorway. "Put that down right now." The color had returned to her face and she was shaking. "How dare you threaten to hit my child! How dare you." Mabel had never seen her mother so angry. "You may pack your bags and leave. I will not tolerate such behavior."

"You won't tolerate such behavior?" Nanny Grimshaw gasped, not letting go of Mabel. "After all I've put up with, looking after this—this charity case for eight years. And I've never said a word, have I?" she spat out. "Oh, I knew," Nanny Grimshaw said, breathing hard. "The Cranfords' nanny was most informative. But I kept it to myself. You should be thanking me for all I've done."

"I'll thank you to leave," Nora said in a low voice, pointing at the front door. "I have clearly been blind about a great many things."

"You'll never find another nanny to take my place. Mabel is ungovernable." Nanny Grimshaw sniffed and pulled back her shoulders. "I was planning on giving my notice anyway. I know she put me under some kind of spell the other night, and I will not stand for such behavior. I've a good mind to report her to Miss Brewer."

"Please go," Nora said sharply. "Now."

The moment Nanny Grimshaw loosened her hold, Mabel yanked her arm free and ran upstairs to her room. She closed the door and banged against it, over and over, until her fist was swollen and throbbing. Then Mabel climbed into bed, burying herself under her feather comforter. It was warm and dark and she never wanted to come out. Shutting her eyes, she hunched into a tight ball, and with tears slipping down her cheeks, Mabel escaped into a shocked sleep.

She slept for a long time, noticing when she woke up, that the light was soft and mellow, full of the golden glow of a summer afternoon. Someone had left a cup of tea and a piece of seedcake on the little table beside her bed. But Mabel wasn't hungry. Tea and cake couldn't fill the emptiness she felt inside her right now.

Somewhere out there she had another mother. Getting out of bed, Mabel went to find Nora.

"I'd like to know the truth, please," Mabel said, standing beside Nora's chair.

Nora nodded and reached for Mabel's hand. "I didn't mean to lie to you, Mabel. I really didn't. But I hated seeing you get hurt. Eliza Cranford was awful to you. All the children were, and when we moved to Potts Bottom, it seemed like the perfect opportunity for a fresh start. I didn't want you being teased at school, or judged. I just wanted to protect you." Nora squeezed Mabel's fingers. "I love you, Mabel."

"Did you really find me in a flowerpot?" Mabel asked, sinking down on the footstool by Nora's chair.

"I did." Nora nodded. And in a soft voice she told Mabel all about her beginnings, about finding her tucked up in one of the terra-cotta flowerpots by the front door, covered in a blanket of ferns.

"How could my mother do that to me?" Mabel whispered.

"It was full of earth and nice and soft. Your mother did it out of love, Mabel. You must believe that. She wanted you to have a better life."

"I don't believe any mother would abandon her baby out of love," Mabel said fiercely.

"If she couldn't take care of you, she had little

choice," Nora murmured. "Otherwise you would have ended up in an orphanage."

Mabel picked at a loose thread on the embroidered stool cover. "Why did she choose your house?" she asked. "Did she know you?"

"I have a feeling that she did. Frank and I spent many afternoons distributing blankets and food to the poor, and after he died I continued on for some years, doing what I could." Nora was silent for a few moments, and then said, "It was well known that Frank and I had wanted children."

For a long time the room was silent. Mabel wrapped her arms around her legs, trying to picture what her mother looked like. Did she ever think of Mabel and wonder what had happened to her? Did she have the same achy feeling in her heart that Mabel was experiencing right now? At one point Nora handed Mabel her handkerchief, and Mabel dabbed at her eyes with it, not realizing she had been crying.

"I pushed Winifred," Mabel said at last. "And I ran out of class. I'm bound to get in a lot of trouble."

"Would you like me to go and talk to Miss Brewer tomorrow? Try and explain things?" Nora said.

"No, thank you," Mabel replied. "I'll manage." She heaved a heavy sigh, listening to the rhythmic ticking of the clock.

"Is Nanny really gone?" Mabel suddenly asked, not quite believing that Nanny Grimshaw wasn't waiting on the other side of the door, ready to march Mabel up to the nursery.

"I should have let her go a long time ago. That was another of my mistakes. I didn't listen to you, and I'm so sorry. You tried to tell me, Mabel. I should have paid more attention. Not been so busy with my roses." Nora put her head in her hands and groaned.

"That's all right, Mama. Nanny was different with you. I'm just glad she's left," Mabel said. "And I don't think we need another nanny."

"No." Nora nodded in agreement. "I believe we can manage without one."

"I think, if you don't mind, I would like to change my name to Magnolia," Mabel said. "Mabel doesn't feel right anymore. Perhaps my real grandmother was called Magnolia? Maybe that's why I have always liked the name." Mabel squeezed her eyes shut.

"Oh, Mabel." Nora's eyes filled with sadness.

"You should have told me," Mabel whispered, pressing her face against her knees. "Mothers don't keep secrets from their daughters."

Lying in bed that evening, Mabel couldn't sleep. She kicked her covers off and then yanked them back on, unable to settle. Somewhere out there she had a mother and a father she had never met. Perhaps it had all been a horrible accident, Mabel thought, flipping her pillow to the cool side. Perhaps she had bounced out of their carriage driving over a pothole one night and they didn't see. Maybe someone found her outside the Ratcliff house and put her in the flowerpot to keep her safe. Maybe her parents never realized she was gone until they got home, and by then it was too late. Maybe they grieved for years and years, not knowing what had happened to her. Mabel's eyes filled with tears, imagining what they might look like. Her father would be tall with kind eyes, and her mother would have the softest hands and the sweetest smile. They would have loved Mabel so much that they never went on to have any more children. Mabel thumped her pillow, and then thumped it again, over and over until tiny feathers leaked out. She dropped her head down and started to sob, knowing in her heart that she had been left in that flowerpot on purpose.

....

Chapter Eighteen

Cobweb-Sweeping Duty and a Brain Wave

IT FELT SO STRANGE THE NEXT MORNING, NOT HAVING Nanny Grimshaw there, flinging back her curtains. And when Mabel washed her face, she realized that Daisy had brought up warm water in the pitcher and not cold. Nora rose early to have breakfast with her, and Daisy had made scones, spread thickly with butter and homemade gooseberry jam.

"I'm never going to make another pan of porridge again as long as I live," Daisy whispered, braiding Mabel's hair for her. "Now that the mean old nanny goat has gone." Mabel knew Daisy was only trying to cheer her up, but she couldn't smile. There was too much to think about, what with Nora not being her real mother, and the thought of facing Miss Brewer and all the girls at school. Mabel's stomach ached. All she wanted was to crawl back into bed.

Nora gave her an extra-long hug before she left. "Miss Brewer is a sensible woman," she pointed out. "I'm sure she won't judge you too harshly."

Ruby was waiting for Mabel outside the house, admiring Nora's magnificent roses. "I thought we could walk to school together," Ruby said, "since you left Lightning and your broomstick behind yesterday. To be honest I'd rather walk than fly, anyway," she added.

"Thanks, Ruby." Mabel tried to keep the glumness from her voice.

The girls walked in silence for a while, Ruby's cat trotting along beside them. It was only as they turned down Glover Lane that Ruby spoke. "No one cares what Winifred said, Mabel. It's not important where you came from. I'm just glad that we're friends."

"It's important to me," Mabel whispered. "Apparently I came from a flowerpot, Ruby."

"Then you were meant to be found by Mrs. Ratcliff," Ruby said firmly. "Because judging from her roses, she is amazing at taking care of things."

Mabel swallowed the lump in her throat. It was impossible to explain how she felt inside. But things were different now, and Mabel couldn't sweep away what she had discovered. Or ignore it. "I've decided to change my name to Magnolia," she said. "Mabel is a family name, and it has never felt right to me."

"Well, I like it," Ruby said stoutly. "I always have. But I'll try and get used to Magnolia," she added quickly, "if that is really what you want."

"It is," Mabel said. "The best news is Nanny Grimshaw has gone. Mama fired her because she tried to beat me." Giving a shaky laugh, Mabel added, "It was almost worth finding out where I came from to be rid of her." But knowing that Nora had kept the truth from her all these years hurt. And turning her head away, Mabel brushed a hand across her eyes.

"So no more cold porridge for breakfast," Ruby said. "That must make you happy."

Mabel nodded, glad that she had Ruby to walk into school with. As soon as Tabitha saw her, she raced over and gave Mabel a long hug.

Feeling ready to face her doom, Mabel walked straight to Miss Brewer's office.

"How nice of you to join us today," Miss Brewer said, folding her hands on her desk.

Mabel wasn't sure if Miss Brewer was being sarcastic or not, but at least she hadn't taken down the whipping wand, which hung from a hook on the wall.

"I apologize for my behavior yesterday," Mabel said. "I should not have pushed Winifred or run away."

"No, you should not, Mabel Ratcliff. That sort of conduct is unacceptable here at Ruthersfield, and we do not tolerate it. When you put on your uniform and walk outside, you represent this school, and young witches do not shove other students. They do not leave class in the middle of a lesson, either."

"I'm sorry, Miss Brewer. I really am."

"Nor," Miss Brewer continued, "do they behave with the petty meanness that Winifred displayed. So you will both spend the morning on cobweb-cleaning duty."

Mabel stared at the headmistress, waiting for her to say more. "Well, go on, Mabel, shoo." Miss Brewer picked up a pen. "I cannot spend all day dealing with your problems."

Sometimes Miss Brewer could be surprisingly human, and as Mabel opened the door, she decided it was worth the risk. "About the flying petition, Miss Brewer?"

"Leave," Miss Brewer said, pointing at the whipping wand. "Before I get that down."

Mabel spent the rest of the morning flying around the school with Lightning, dusting all the cobwebs from the corners. She tried to keep out of Winifred's way, but at one point they both found themselves sweeping the great hall together. Surprisingly, Winifred didn't say anything to Mabel, and at lunchtime Mabel noticed that her eyes looked all red from crying. Diana and Florence kept hovering over her, patting Winifred's back and murmuring things in her ears. Mabel asked Ruby and Tabitha if they knew what the matter was.

"Diana told me that Winifred's upset because she doesn't want to let her father down," Ruby said. "Apparently he's expecting her to enter the competition and win. At least that's what Winifred told Diana."

"Maybe that's why she's been so horrid lately?" Tabitha said. "Because she's worried about the competition. And she's taking it out on you."

"I thought she might have felt bad about being so mean," Mabel sighed. "But clearly not." And by the end of the day, apart from her puffy eyes, Winifred was back to her confident, bragging self.

"I think Winifred has never forgiven me for getting that glamorizing spell right in year one," Mabel said, flying part of the way home with Ruby after school. At the bottom of Canal Street, Ruby would veer off down the path toward her cottage, and Mabel would fly on to Trotting Hill.

"She's scared of you," Ruby replied, swerving a little as she flew.

"Winifred! Scared of me! That's ridiculous. She's beautiful and elegant and —"

"Especially now," Ruby broke in, "since she knows you're going to come up with something wonderful and Mabelish for the competition, and she won't."

"Magnoliaish, and I haven't decided on anything yet," Mabel said. "Although now that Nanny Grimshaw's gone, I'll have much more time to work on it."

"I'm trying to make cloud slippers for my ma," Ruby said. "Her feet hurt her all the time, and with cloud slippers she could feel like she's walking on air. But clouds are so hard to work with. They keep falling apart, so I'll have to chose something else."

"I'm working on a hair-growing potion, but that's not going very well either," Mabel said, deciding to ask Daisy if she might have another go at experimenting when she got home.

"Absolutely not," Daisy said, shaking her head. She was hanging laundry on the line. Mabel opened her mouth to speak, but Daisy cut her off before she could say anything else on the subject. "No more messing about with my hair, thank you very much."

Mabel sighed and sank onto the grass next to

Lightning, who immediately rolled over to get his belly stroked.

"Not a drop of wind," Daisy muttered, pegging out Nora's emerald dress. "And your mother wanted to wear this to one of her meetings tomorrow. It's never going to dry at this rate." Mabel sighed again, louder this time. "So how was school?" Daisy asked, as she hung up a pair of bloomers.

"Not as bad as I thought it would be." Mabel's voice grew tight and her chest ached. "But I just can't believe I'm an orphan, Daisy. That my mother abandoned me."

"Miss Mabel," Daisy said, before Mabel quickly interrupted her.

"It's Magnolia now, remember?"

Daisy rolled her eyes. "Doesn't matter what your name is. Nora took you in and gave you a home. She loved you from the moment she set eyes on you. You should be very grateful to her. She's as much your mother as the woman who birthed you."

"Except I can't stop thinking about what my other mother was like. Why she did what she did." Mabel plucked at the grass. "I feel lost, Daisy, like I don't know where I belong anymore."

"That's the shock of finding out," Daisy said sensibly. "But you do know where you belong. Right here."

"Nora's not my real family though, is she?"

"Don't be ridiculous," Daisy said bluntly. "Families are the people who look after us and love us. You and Mrs. Ratcliff are like family to me. I never knew my own parents, and that's just the way it is."

A deep wave of loneliness swept over Mabel. Daisy hadn't heard what she was saying. It didn't feel ridiculous to Mabel, wanting to know her own story.

"Now, how about a cup of tea and a bun," Daisy said more gently, "since this dress isn't going to dry with me gawking at it."

Mabel looked up and blinked. She took off her glasses and brushed away her tears, staring at Daisy.

"What is it?" Daisy asked suspiciously. "Something's going on in that head of yours. I can tell."

Mabel scrambled to her feet and gave a watery smile. "I think you have just given me an idea, Daisy."

"So long as it doesn't concern my hair," Daisy said, protectively touching her cap. "It's finally starting to grow back in."

"No, it doesn't. But I know what I'm going to make for the competition." Mabel waved at the line of laundry. "What if you could have a drying spell in a bottle?"

"I'm not following," Daisy said. "At all."

"Well, supposing you want your clothes to dry and there's no wind, or it's a rainy day and you have to hang them inside," Mabel explained a little breath-lessly. "Imagine how much simpler life would be if you opened a bottle and a warm breeze blew out and dried them all for you."

"I'll say," Daisy said with a laugh. "No more wet clothes dripping all over the floor in the winter. But how on earth could you do that?"

"I think it might be possible." Mabel cleaned her glasses on her pinafore. "I'd need to collect some strong warm winds, which could be a little challenging," she confessed. "Wind isn't an easy ingredient to work with. But I have my guide to spell construction. I'm sure I can do it."

"Are you now?" Daisy hitched the empty laundry basket onto her hip. "And where would you get this wind from?" she asked, glancing up at the sky. "Potts Bottom doesn't seem to have much blowing around lately."

"Somewhere like Melton Bay," Mabel answered. "Remember those hot summery breezes that would gust in off the ocean?" She spread her arms out wide and spun around. "I'd have to collect lots of sample winds to see which strength worked best, and then construct a simple spell to go along with it."

"Why don't you stick to something easier," Daisy said, "that doesn't involve wind?"

"I do have another idea to make your hair grow." Mabel lowered her voice and whispered. "We could try rubbing toad's blood all over your head. Toad's blood is great for making tomatoes grow to twice their normal size."

"Go with the wind," Daisy said, heading toward the house.

Chapter Nineteen

....

A Trip to Melton Bay

WHEN MABEL TOLD RUBY ABOUT HER DRYING SPELL idea the next day, Ruby grabbed Mabel's arm in excitement.

"My pa is taking us all to the beach on Sunday. We're getting the train to Melton Bay. Why don't you come with us? I'm sure Ma wouldn't mind. Then you could collect your wind samples."

"Oh, Ruby, that's a marvelous idea, and if we both say sun spells on Saturday evening, we should be certain of getting good weather."

Miss Mantel talked to the girls in potions class that afternoon, going over the basic rules of spell construction and how to approach the competition. She reminded them to use ingredients they were familiar with and had worked with before. "Draw on the knowledge you already have," Miss Mantel told the class. "And remember to always refer to your handbooks. There is a compatibility list at the back. Some ingredients do not mix well with others, and it's important to make sure that all parts of your spell work together. Be sensible, girls."

Nora was a little hesitant to let Mabel go to the seaside at first, even when Mabel told her that she needed to collect wind for her invention.

"But why does it have to be Melton Bay?" Nora asked. "There are lots of other seaside towns along the coast."

"Because this is where Ruby's family wants to go. And I'd like to see where I came from," Mabel admitted, not sure why this felt important to her, but it did.

"Well, I suppose a day out will do you good," Nora sighed.

Early on Sunday morning she gave Mabel a shilling for the train ride and the cost of an ice cream, and Daisy packed a bag of ham sandwiches to contribute to the Tanners' picnic. Mabel had decided to keep her competition idea a secret, and apart from Ruby, Daisy, and Nora, she hadn't told anyone else. Especially as Mabel had a sneaking suspicion that if the teachers knew she was attempting to harvest wind, they might try to stop her. Miss Mantel did know she was collecting something, because Mabel had asked for permission to use the little glass bottles that were kept in the potions room. "Just make sure you bring them all back when you have finished with your experiment," Miss Mantel had said. "I'll be curious to see what you come up with, Mabel."

The Tanners had arranged for Bill Moor, a farmer who lived just outside Potts Bottom, to take them all to the train station in his hay wagon. They were collecting Mabel on the way, and she was waiting outside when they pulled up, clutching her broomstick and satchel of bottles. Luckily, Nora, who wasn't fully awake yet, hadn't thought to ask Mabel why she was taking her broomstick but not her cat to the beach, since she wasn't allowed to fly without him. Before she could ask, Mabel quickly climbed into the back of the wagon to join Ruby and her sisters, all dressed in clean pinafores and sunbonnets, giggling with the thrill of a day out at the sea. Mr. and Mrs. Tanner sat up front with Farmer Moor, looking stiff and formal in their smart Sunday clothes, the baby perched on Mrs. Tanner's lap.

It was a bumpy ride, and the cart swayed and bounced as they trotted along, winding through the lanes toward Little Shamlington. Farmer Moor's horse started to whinny right before Mabel heard the distant roar of an engine behind them. It got louder and louder, and she glanced back to see the Delacy car speeding in their direction, its headlights looking like the huge glaring eyes of a mechanical beast. The car overtook them as they rounded a corner, forcing the hay wagon into the ditch. Mr. Tanner said something that would have gotten his mouth washed out with soap if Daisy had heard, and Mrs. Tanner clutched at her youngest daughter, who almost flew out of the cart. Mabel saw Winifred peer around at them as the horse lumbered back onto the road.

But even Winifred Delacy couldn't ruin such a beautiful day. Ruby and Mabel's sun spells had worked, and Mabel felt like a roasting chestnut as they crowded into the steam train at Little Shamlington. She sat next to the window, squished up against Ruby. Mabel was quiet on the journey, staring out at the fields and villages that flashed by, her good mood tinged with an edge of melancholy. When they pulled into Melton Bay, Mabel felt a little dizzy as she stood up, from the memories as well as the heat.

It was strange, walking through the streets as a tourist, following the stream of day-trippers heading toward the beach. A lady wearing a lavender gown and glasses strolled past. She had freckles across her nose and flyaway brown hair, and for an instant Mabel wondered if this might be her mother. She wanted to reach out and touch the woman's skirt, see if they recognized each other. But the woman had already gone, leaving Mabel with a deep sense of yearning. She stopped at the end of Oak Lane and rested against a streetlamp. "Do you mind if I just go up here for a moment?" she asked Mrs. Tanner. "It's where I used to live. Number Fourteen, Oak Lane."

"Go right ahead. We'll wait for you," Mrs. Tanner said, handing baby Eva to Ruby and fanning herself with her hand. "My, it is hot."

Mabel knew what she was looking for as she stood in front of the redbrick house that used to be her home. She stared for a long moment at the two large terra-cotta flowerpots that sat on either side of the doorway, overflowing with purple petunias. Without quite realizing what she was doing, Mabel walked up the path and crouched down, wrapping her arms around one of the flowerpots. It was warm from the sun, and Mabel stuck her hand in, touching soft earth. A tear slid down her cheek and splashed onto a flower, as Mabel imagined her mother leaving her there. How could anyone do such a thing? How could she? Picking up a stone, Mabel flung it as hard as she could, hitting the wall of the house opposite. Then taking off her glasses, she used her sleeve to wipe her eyes so the Tanners wouldn't notice she had been crying. For a few moments Mabel crouched in a fuzzy haze, the world all blurry and out of focus. But she couldn't hide here forever, and slipping her glasses back on, Mabel stood up and walked back along the lane to join the others.

The pier was crowded. Mabel could hear the organ grinder playing, and bursts of laughter came from the direction of the Punch and Judy show. It was as if she had stepped back into the past. Memories flooded her as they climbed down onto the beach. As soon as Ruby's little sisters saw the donkey rides, they started jumping up and down. "Please, Ma, please, Pa. May we have a go?"

Mr. Tanner put the picnic hamper down on the sand, and with his small daughters hanging on to his hands, led them off toward the donkeys.

"Can we take a walk?" Mabel whispered to Ruby. "I need to find somewhere quiet." She nodded along the beach. "Not many people used to go beyond those rocks."

"I'll have to ask Ma," Ruby said. "She may insist Beatrice comes with us." But the sun and sea air had made Mrs. Tanner most agreeable, and she waved the girls off with a smile.

"Don't go too far now, and stay together."

"What's the broom for?" Beatrice asked from under her parasol.

"The broom?" Mabel repeated, swallowing nervously.

"I'm just teasing you," Beatrice said. "Don't look so worried, Mabel. If I were a witch, I'd keep my broomstick with me all the time. I'd sleep with it in our bed like Ruby does, tickling my feet with the bristles!"

"Not always." Ruby glared at her sister. "Only the first night I got it."

"Go on with you now," Mrs. Tanner said, flapping her hands at them and settling herself back on a blanket. "Enough chitter chatter. I deserve a little peace and quiet."

Mabel led Ruby down the beach. There were groups of children making sand castles, and even though Mabel knew that Eliza Cranford probably wore her hair up and her skirts down by now, she couldn't help scanning the faces of the sand castle builders, looking for Eliza's cruel smile. Once they got past the rocky outcrop at the end of the public beach, Mabel hurried around the point, red faced and sweating.

"Good, there's no one here," she panted, untying her pinafore.

"What are you doing?" Ruby asked in alarm.

"Trying out my trousers," Mabel said, tugging off her dress and petticoats and exposing the trousers she had made in sewing class. "Gosh, I was hot under here!"

"Mabel!" Ruby gasped in horror. "You look like a boy!"

"I still have my braids," Mabel said, giving a little skip. "But I've got so much more freedom."

"My mother would faint if she saw you," Ruby said.

Mabel picked up her broomstick and slung the satchel of bottles over her shoulder. "If I'm going to fly about collecting wind, I can't risk falling off into the ocean." She flung a leg over her broomstick. "This way I'll have more control."

"What if someone sees you?" Ruby said.

"People may think it a little strange, but they're not going to report me to the police or anything. It's a Ruthersfield rule I'm breaking, not a law." Ruby shook her head, but she was smiling as Mabel swooped into the air.

Carefully lifting one hand off the broomstick, Mabel pulled a bottle out of the bag. The breeze dropped as she tugged the cork out with her teeth and scooped up some of the wind. Using her mouth, Mabel immediately stuck the cork back in and, still hovering, grabbed the pencil from her trouser pocket and wrote a number 1 on the label. Tucking the bottle into the bag, Mabel removed another and waited for the breeze to pick up a little. As soon as it did, she pulled out the cork and trapped some of the air inside. Mabel wrote a 2 on this bottle. For the stronger winds she flew farther out, dipping and diving and catching the gusts in her bottles. Depending on the strength of the wind, she would write down the corresponding number.

It was difficult to stop her glasses from slipping down her nose, and she had to keep tilting her head back to slide them into place. The wind was gusting fiercely as Mabel held up the last bottle, almost knocking her off her broomstick. She gave a soft cry of fear and her hand shook as she wrote a wobbly number 10 on the label. Turning her broomstick around, Mabel flew shakily back to shore.

"I thought you were going to fall off," Ruby said, as Mabel landed on the sand beside her.

"Me too," Mabel panted. "I would have if I'd been riding sidesaddle."

"How was it?" Ruby said. "It looked so dangerous."

Mabel smiled at her friend. "That is the only way to ride a broomstick, Ruby!"

Chapter Twenty

Good Works

THE REST OF THE DAY WAS ONE MABEL WOULD NEVER forget. She enjoyed being part of a big noisy family, although it was impossible to ignore the feeling that somewhere close by might be her mother. A shadow mother that hovered over her while she paddled in the ocean, and sat beside her while she ate the picnic Mrs. Tanner spread out. And when Mabel bought an ice cream from the vendor on the pier to share with Ruby, she wondered if her mother had ever tasted such a treat, creamy like custard and cold as snow.

On the train ride home Mabel fell asleep. Her face was sore with sunburn and her braids had come unraveled. She didn't wake up until Ruby gently shook her when they arrived in Little Shamlington. Farmer Moor was waiting with his horse and cart, and Mabel stumbled into the hay wagon, along with the Tanner girls. She leaned against Ruby, staring up at the wide star-filled sky. "One day," Mabel murmured, "I want to catch the stars and use their power to fuel the world. Like this new electricity everyone is talking about, but bigger, better."

"And how will you do that, Mabel?" Ruby said with a yawn.

"I don't know," Mabel replied. "But don't you get the shivers just looking at all that space, wondering what's up there? I want to invent a broomstick to fly to the moon."

The Tanner girls laughed at this, and Mr. Tanner turned around. "You are a dreamer, Mabel," he said, and then softly added, "It's good to have dreams."

Nora and Daisy were waiting up for her when she got home. After a cup of warm posset—hot milk flavored with treacle—Mabel fell straight into bed, relieved that Nanny Grimshaw wasn't there to insist she brush her hair one hundred times first.

"Did you get your wind samples?" Nora asked, smoothing the patchwork quilt over her.

Mabel nodded, too tired to speak. "And ice cream," she mumbled. "So delicious!" Nora smiled, and before she had even left the room, Mabel was fast asleep.

Getting up for school the next day wasn't easy. Daisy had to shake her three times. "You need to get going, Miss Mabel."

"Magnolia," Mabel murmured sleepily.

"If you can't get yourself up and dressed, then your mama may think about hiring a new nanny." That sent Mabel scrambling out of bed. There was no way she was going to risk having another Nanny Grimshaw in the house.

Mabel had completely forgotten about the good works program they were starting that afternoon, until Miss Seymour announced it in class. Ruthersfield put a great deal of emphasis on its girls helping out in the community, and although there were some groans from a few of the students, Mabel was delighted to escape having to work on her knitting project, a pointed black wool nightcap with a floppy brim that looked more like a squashed porcupine than something you'd wear to bed.

"Florence and Winifred, you will be offering assistance at the soup kitchen," Miss Seymour said. "And Diana and Tabitha, you are both going to be working with Helping Hands." Helping Hands was an organization of witches that spent time visiting the sick in hospitals. They would sit quietly beside patients, resting their hands on broken bones and wounds and using their healing powers to speed up recovery. The Helping Hands witches wore red and purple capes with the healing hands insignia on the front, a pair of hands clasped around a witch's hat. They were known for their beauty and style, and patients were always falling in love with them.

"Miss Seymour, please," Winifred said. "Might I do Helping Hands instead of the soup kitchen? I feel I would be much better suited for it."

"I'm afraid not, Winifred," Miss Seymour replied briskly. She turned to Mabel and Ruby. "You girls will be taking the stew pot and puppet show along to the orphanage."

"How appropriate," Winifred muttered under her breath.

Mabel bit her lip. She would not give Winifred the satisfaction of seeing her upset.

"Why don't you report her to Miss Brewer?" Ruby said, as the girls walked into town behind their group leader, Violet Featherstone. There were three other students doing the orphanage visit. One of them carried the stew pot, and Mabel carried the box of puppets.

"It's not worth reporting Winifred," Mabel sighed. "Her dad is on the board of governors and nothing will ever happen to her. I'll just get in trouble," she said. "Besides, I don't like to be a tattletale. I can deal with Winifred."

"Excuse me?" Violet Featherstone turned around, giving Mabel and Ruby the full benefit of her icy glare. "A lady talks in a quiet voice. She doesn't gossip like a fishwife."

"When I grow up," Mabel murmured to Ruby, "I intend to slouch in my chairs, never wear bonnets, talk about whatever I like, and laugh at the top of my lungs."

"How unladylike!" Ruby whispered back, and the two girls had to stuff their hands in their mouths to try to muffle their giggles.

The Potts Bottom Orphanage was next door to the elementary school. They were both rather gloomy redbrick buildings with narrow windows and gray slate roofs. Some of the older children from the orphanage were allowed to attend the school, and Mabel watched as a line of girls filed out one door and a line of boys filed out another, all heading home for lunch. The orphan children trooped back around to the orphanage in a ragged group, their hair tangled and their clothes worn. Tagging along behind, they looked greedily at the stew pot as Violet led the Ruthersfield girls inside.

It was the silence that upset Mabel the most. She had been expecting noise and screaming, considering all the children who were housed in here, but the orphanage was strangely quiet. Rows of cribs held little children and babies. The ones who could stand leaned over the side of their cribs, stretching their arms out to be picked up, while the babies lay on their backs, staring at the ceiling and sucking their thumbs. There were no books or toys for the children to play with, and Mabel cringed as a large woman in a black dress and white cap swept through the room, herding the children into a line. "One at a time," she ordered gruffly.

The children lined up as Violet waved her wand over the stew pot. "Swellifanto," she called out in her musical voice. A cloud of fragrant steam puffed out of the pot, and Violet handed Mabel the spoon. "You can fill their bowls," she said, and as the children filed past Mabel, she dolloped a big spoonful of stew into each wooden bowl. It smelled delicious and looked to be full of carrots and onions and big chunks of mutton. The children stared at Mabel out of huge, hungry eyes, their faces grimy with dirt. Most of them were barefoot, and the ones wearing shoes had string tied around them to keep them on. Mabel spooned out stew in silence. She had never seen anything so sad.

"Can we have more?" a little boy asked, holding out his bowl for a second spoonful.

"Of course you can," Mabel whispered, hoping she wouldn't get him into trouble. "There's plenty of stew."

"Does it always make the same kind?" Ruby asked Violet.

"No, you never know what you're going to get. That is a very temperamental stew pot," Violet said. "Sometimes it's chicken stew, sometimes pork. Last week the poor children had to make do with bean and turnip." Violet gave a shudder of disgust. "That smelled so nasty."

When the children had finished eating, they gathered on the floor at one end of the room, and Violet opened the box of puppets. "What shall we give them?" she asked the other Ruthersfield girls. "'The Snow Queen'? 'The Princess and the Pea'? 'The Little Mermaid'?"

"'The Princess and the Pea,'" Mabel said.

Waving her wand over the box, Violet called out, "Puppetito showiso—'Princess and the Pea.'"

The box flew open and out danced the puppets. There were the princess and the prince, the king and queen, and into the air floated a bed with about twenty little mattresses piled up on top. Mabel watched the children's faces more than the puppet show. They were transfixed by the dolls that were dancing and acting out the fairy tale in front of them. When it was over the children clapped in appreciation, and one little girl, who couldn't have been more than five, ran over to Mabel and wrapped her arms around Mabel's legs. "Stay," she begged. "More stew and more show."

"Come along now," the woman in charge said, pulling the little girl off Mabel. "Aren't you supposed to be working in the laundry, Ann? Off you go." And she pushed the child toward the door.

Mabel was silent on the way back to Ruthersfield. She hugged the warm stew pot against her, thinking how different her life would have been if Nora hadn't taken her in. She might have ended up in a place just like that, and Mabel's heart ached for the children who didn't have anyone else to love them.

Chapter Twenty-One

....

The Ratcliff Family Tree

D O YOU THINK MY MOTHER WAS A WITCH?" MABEL asked at tea that afternoon. She was sitting with Nora in the drawing room, on one of the slippery horsehair sofas. Daisy had made a seedcake and a plate of cucumber sandwiches.

Nora looked at Mabel and said carefully, "I doubt it, Mabel dear. I mean Magnolia," she corrected herself. "Witches usually have skills that can help them survive, and I got the feeling your mother was desperate. She didn't have anyone else to turn to. If she ended up in the poorhouse, they would have taken you from her, and no mother could bear that for her child."

"Would I have been sent to the orphanage?" Mabel said. "Like the one in Potts Bottom that we visited today?"

"I think there's a strong chance that you would have been." Nora poured herself out more tea. "I truly believe your mother gave you up because she wished you to have a better life. Because she loved you, not because she didn't want you."

Mabel pulled a slice of cucumber out of her sandwich and ate it. Her lip trembled. "I wish I knew more about where I came from," she said. Her voice cracked as she looked up at Nora and said, "I'm never going to find my mother, am I?"

"I'm afraid you probably won't," Nora said. And then more softly, "But I'm your mother too, Mabel. I might not have given birth to you, but I love you like a mother."

Mabel sighed. "It's just that the girls at school are always bringing up their witch ancestors, and I know nothing about mine. Who the witches in my family were."

Nora didn't reply right away. "I wish I had those answers for you," she said at last. "But I don't. I can't fill in all the pieces, and that breaks my heart."

"So I'll never know, will I?"

"Not about your birth family," Nora said, getting up

from the sofa. She walked across to her desk, returning with a rolled up piece of paper. "But these are also your roots, Magnolia." Mabel had to admit that even though she loved the name Magnolia, it didn't sound right when her mother said it. Nora put the tea tray down on the floor and unrolled the piece of paper across the delicate walnut table. Mabel saw it was a family tree.

"But that's the Ratcliff's family tree, not mine," Mabel said.

"You're a Ratcliff too," Nora insisted. "I gave you my husband's name, and had he been alive when I found you, he would have welcomed you into our little family." Nora ran her hands over the paper. "There may not be witches in the Ratcliff family, but there were some strong-minded women," she said, smiling at Mabel. "A lot like you and me." Circling the name Irene Ratcliff, she said, "Now, it's rumored that Irene ran off to sea and became a pirate. Quite a woman if the stories about her are true."

"Can we call her a witch?" Mabel said. "She might have been one, don't you think? Maybe she had the gift very mildly. Maybe she didn't even know."

"Maybe," Nora agreed, smiling. She bent down and circled Rachel Ratcliff. "Look, we can go right back to the thirteenth century. Rachel Ratcliff was an amazing woman. She mixed herbs and gave them to the sick.

Frank did some research on her at one time."

"Oh, she sounds like a witch too, doesn't she?" Mabel said. "It's just"—and her throat grew tight—"I hate feeling like an outsider. Like I don't belong."

Nora took a deep breath. "You're not an outsider. Look, here you are." She gestured at the paper with her pen, hesitating a moment. "Do I write down Mabel or Magnolia?"

"Well, I still wish you had called me Magnolia," Mabel sighed, "because it is a beautiful name and it suits me so much better. But I think you should write Mabel," she said at last. "Even though it's plain and not very pretty, I'm glad you named me after your mother."

Nora smiled, and under "Frank Ratcliff married to Nora Darling—1867," she wrote "Mabel Ratcliff, daughter of Nora and Frank Ratcliff—1887." She rolled the piece of parchment back up and handed it to Mabel. Her eyes glistened. "I can't give you everything you're looking for, Mabel, but I want you to have this. Because you are a part of this family."

"I know that," Mabel said. "I know," she said again. "I just wish I had something to connect me to my other family too."

"You have your magic, Mabel. No one can take that away from you." Nora gave a shaky laugh. "That is something you most certainly didn't get from any of us!"

"Why did you take me in?" Mabel asked softly. "Did you feel sorry for me?"

"I took you in because I had always longed for a baby." Nora's jaw tightened. "Take no notice of those awful things Nanny Grimshaw said." She slumped back in her chair and closed her eyes. "That is one of my biggest regrets. Not getting rid of Nanny sooner. I should have done a lot of things differently." She was quiet for so long Mabel wondered if her mother had gone to sleep, but then Nora said, "I should have told you the truth from the beginning, Mabel. I'm so sorry. I just wanted you to feel loved."

Mabel had never heard her mother sound so sad. She got up and walked around the table, bending down to give her a hug. "I do feel loved."

There was a knock on the door, and Daisy came in to clear the tea things. "You can call me Mabel again, Daisy, if you like," Mabel announced. "I love the name Magnolia. I always will," she said wistfully. "But since Mama christened me Mabel, I've decided to keep it."

"Well, I'm happy to hear that," Daisy grunted, picking up the tray.

After tea, Mabel took her satchel of wind samples and *Simple Guide to Spell Construction* out into the garden. The ache in her chest wasn't quite so sharp, and she settled herself on the grass, breathing in the heavy scent of Nora's roses. Most of the bushes were in full bloom. The Royal Duchesses definitely had the most powerful smell, and Mabel decided that she would crush some of the deep red petals and add them to her dryer spell. But first she needed to test the strength of her wind samples, which made her a little nervous, because under the directory of ingredients at the back of Miss Tate's booklet, it said, "Wind is a highly sensitive element in spells and must be handled with extreme care. Contained wind is a volatile substance and should only be used by the advanced witch."

Well, she would be extremely careful and start with one of the gentler winds. Then once she had the correct strength down, she could figure out how to make the spell blow for a twenty-minute cycle. That should be enough time to dry most clothes, and if you had heavy blankets on your line, you could simply let another cycle out of the bottle. Mabel pushed her glasses up her nose. Perhaps each bottle could hold ten drying cycles?

Scrambling off the grass, she ran to the back door and poked her head into the kitchen. Lightning was asleep on the windowsill, and the sweet smell of sugar and strawberries announced that Daisy was making jam. She stood at the stove, stirring a long wooden spoon around the big copper pot, a cloud of sweet steam scenting the room.

"Is it all right if I experiment with those sheets on the line, Daisy? I need to test out the strength of my drying spell."

"So long as you don't get them dirty," Daisy said. "They're the good linen ones from your mother's bed. It took me an age to wash them and put them through the mangle."

"Thanks." Mabel raced off before Daisy changed her mind.

She decided to start with a number five wind. Her strongest sample was a ten and her weakest a number one, so five seemed like a good place to start. Taking one of the bottles from her satchel, Mabel pulled out the cork. Immediately a blast of warm wind shot out, tugging the sheets right off the line. "Oh, not good," Mabel gasped, trying to grab at them. But the wind was far too strong. The laundry tumbled and swirled through the air, catching in the branches of the apple tree. Before Daisy could discover what had happened, Mabel snuck her broomstick out of the house, swung her leg over, and flew up into the tree. Hovering like Miss Reed had taught them, she gently untangled the sheets, praying that Daisy was too busy making jam to look through the window. With her heart racing,

Mabel carried the damp bundle of laundry back down. Quickly, she hung them up again and tried with a number four wind. This one was still too strong. The sheets blew off the line and landed in Daisy's vegetable patch. Hanging them up for a second time, Mabel couldn't help noticing that the snowy white linen was now streaked and smudged with dirt. Well, she would worry about that problem later, Mabel decided, opening a number three. This time she was thrilled to see the clothes puffing on the line as the warm wind blew around them.

"Perfect," Mabel sighed in satisfaction, taking off her glasses and polishing them on her pinafore. The world immediately went fuzzy, and she squinted at the blurry shape marching out the kitchen door.

"What have you been doing?" Daisy shouted. "Those sheets are a disgrace."

"I'm so sorry, Daisy, I really am." Bravely slipping her glasses back on, Mabel saw the full horror on Daisy's face. "But I've made great progress with my invention."

"At the expense of my sheets," Daisy fumed. "Science might be about getting your hands dirty, but not my sheets. Now, do you know any washing spells?"

"I'm afraid I don't," Mabel admitted.

"Then we will just have to do it the old-fashioned

way. Unpeg those linens and bring them through to the kitchen, please."

Even though Mabel had to spend the next hour scrubbing sheets and rolling them through the mangle to squeeze the water out, she really didn't mind because her invention was coming along nicely. A warm wind, combined with rose essence and a timing spell, and Mabel was starting to believe she might actually have discovered a way to dry clothes from a bottle.

Chapter Twenty-Two

....

Success

THAT NIGHT MABEL DREAMED SHE WAS LIVING IN THE orphanage. Instead of ladling out stew, she stood in line with the other children, holding up her bowl to be filled. When she awoke, Mabel was shivering with cold, her covers slumped in a heap on the floor. For a few moments she lay still, watching the pale dawn light creep through the window, relieved it had only been a dream. The clock on the bureau ticked softly, and her breathing began to slow down. She could smell the sweet, buttery scent of Daisy's breakfast scones baking and feel the warm weight of Lightning, curled up by her feet. Nora was asleep next door, and a deep sense of peace washed over Mabel. Climbing out of bed, she went straight to her mother's room.

Nora smiled up at her sleepily. "It's so early, Mabel. What's the matter?"

"I've been thinking," Mabel said. "We could fit at least five more beds in my room, Mama. Ruby shares with five of her sisters, and I wouldn't mind sharing one bit. It'd be cozy."

Nora smothered a yawn. "And who are you planning on sharing with?"

"I was hoping we could adopt some of the orphan children from the village," Mabel said, staring intently at her mother. She could hear a bird chirping outside. "I'd help Daisy with the extra laundry and cooking and things."

"Oh, Mabel." Nora was silent for a long moment. "That is such a sweet idea, but it would never work. It just isn't practical."

"We could try and make it work. Please, Mama, think about it. Talk to Daisy. You took me in."

Nora reached out and touched Mabel's cheek. "I will think about it, I promise. But sometimes you just have to let life be." She sighed. "You can't fix everything, Mabel."

"I can try," Mabel said, her voice quivering. "And I'm

going to ask Miss Brewer if we can visit the orphanage every week. Once a month isn't nearly enough."

But when Mabel proposed her idea, Miss Brewer refused to even consider it.

"You girls are here to study the magical arts," she snapped. "Which is what you should be focusing on."

A lot of the girls at school had given up on their inventions. "It's too hard," Diana Mansfield sighed in cookery class one day. The girls had just finished learning how to make a surprise cake, which, when you cut into it, sent little sugar doves flying out. The doves sang the national anthem, and it was a favorite parlor game for guests to try to catch the doves and eat them. Winifred's doves had stuck to the inside of the cake, so when she cut into it, there was just a sad chirping, but no little birds flew out. Mabel's, on the other hand, sent a great show of doves swooping around the cookery room.

"My father says women's brains aren't designed to invent things," Diana said, catching one of Mabel's doves and popping it into her mouth. "That's for the men to do."

"Well, now, I certainly don't agree with that," Miss Seymour said rather crisply. She was wearing a badge pinned to her cloak with "SOFTW" written across it, which all the girls now knew stood for the Society of Forward-Thinking Witches. Mabel had seen Miss Brewer glaring at the badge in morning assembly, wrinkling up her nose as if it was giving off an unpleasant smell, and Mabel got the feeling that she didn't approve. "Women shouldn't be stopped from doing something they are perfectly capable of, just because they are women," Miss Seymour said. "Remember what Angelina Tate told us, girls: 'Dare to push boundaries and fly against the wind.'" Her gaze swept around the classroom. "I do hope some of you will be entering the competition."

Mabel noticed that Winifred was staring at her, and her eyes looked suspiciously puffy, as if she'd been crying again. Even though she was the most insufferable person Mabel had ever met, she couldn't help feeling a little sorry for Winifred, especially if her father was expecting her to come up with an amazing invention.

"How is your invention coming along?" Mabel asked Ruby as they washed up their cake pans.

"Oh, not good," Ruby sighed. "I'm working on an everlasting candle, but it keeps burning out. I put in oil of unicorn, which is used in the everlasting love potion, so that should keep it burning, but"—Ruby shrugged—"I just don't know what I'm doing wrong."

"Try doubling the amount of unicorn oil," Mabel suggested. "Wax is thick, so you might need more oil to balance the spell out."

"Now, why didn't I think of that?" Ruby said, smiling. "And what's happening with your wind spell?" she whispered.

"I'm going to test it one last time tonight," Mabel said, "so I'll be ready."

Miss Brewer had spoken to the whole school that morning, announcing that not only would members from SOFTW be present for the competition, but the Ruthersfield board of governors would also be in attendance, along with the Potts Bottom mayor and a number of other local dignitaries. "This will be a big day for our school," Miss Brewer had said. "A big day in our history, and I expect every one of you girls to behave in a fitting manner."

Mabel had spent hours perfecting her invention, mixing a number three wind with a teaspoon of crushed dragonfly wings (for a fluttering motion), rabbit breath for softness, rose essence for fragrance, and some ground shell of a ninety-seven-year-old tortoise for stability. To get the timing right she had mixed the spell for exactly twenty minutes and poured the whole thing back into the bottle. It was now sitting on her bureau along with the rest of the wind samples, which

Mabel planned to hand over to Miss Mantel as soon as she could. The potions teacher had been out sick with a summer cold the past few days, so Mabel had drawn little stars on the number ten label, as a warning to herself to handle with extreme care.

As soon as school was over, Mabel flew straight home. Trying to keep her broomstick level was harder than ever since Lightning had put on weight, due to all the stolen kippers he'd been eating. After a currant bun and a glass of milk, Mabel rounded up Nora and Daisy and ushered them into the garden for her big demonstration.

"Now, what you are about to see will amaze and delight you," Mabel said, copying the way the Melton Bay street performers sounded. She waved her hands at the wet laundry hanging on the clothesline. "Imagine this, ladies. You have a fancy party to go to but your favorite bloomers are still wet."

"Oh, my, what a disaster," Daisy gasped, covering her mouth and making Mabel start to giggle. Nora frowned slightly, in disapproval of the word "bloomers," Mabel guessed, but she could see her mother biting her lip to stop herself from smiling.

"Well, all you need is some of this," Mabel said, uncorking the little bottle. A swirl of wind gusted out, tinted pale pink and smelling powerfully of Royal Duchess roses. Mabel shoved the cork back in the bottle, and for the next twenty minutes (timed to the second by Nora's locket watch), they watched the breeze gently blow the clothes on the line back and forth.

"It is warm," Nora said. "I can feel it against my face. I'm so proud of you, Mabel."

"Thank you, Mama." Mabel smiled, a lump swelling in her throat. Would her shadow mother have been proud too, knowing that Mabel was magic?

"Slightly salty," Daisy commented. "But that won't affect the clothes," she reassured Mabel. "A sea breeze does wonders for laundry."

When the twenty minutes were up, the pink breeze evaporated away, leaving Nora's dress and undergarments warm, dry, and scented with roses.

Daisy just kept shaking her head in wonder. "I'm not going to dread wash day anymore," she said. "Honestly, Miss Mabel, I'm in shock, I really am. No more wet clothes dripping all over the floor on rainy Wednesdays."

"I hope the committee likes it," Mabel said, giving a nervous hop. "Do you think I should wear my trousers tomorrow, since some women from the Society of Forward-Thinking Witches will be there? Maybe they would be interested to see how much easier it is to fly a broomstick without petticoats." Mabel continued. "Perhaps I could enter my trousers as a second invention?"

"I wouldn't push too hard, Mabel dear; one boundary at a time," Nora said.

The last thing Mabel wanted was to upset Miss Brewer. But since her mother and Daisy both seemed to be in good moods, Mabel brought up the subject of the orphans.

"Oh, Mabel, I really don't think it can happen," Nora sighed. "We are just not equipped to take in a houseful of children."

"What do you think, Daisy?" Mabel asked.

"Well, we weren't equipped for you, Miss Mabel, but we managed just fine. Of course we certainly couldn't manage a houseful," Daisy said, glancing in Nora's direction, "but you are getting older, Miss Mabel, and I do miss having a little one around."

"We will talk about this later," Nora said, starting to walk toward the house.

"Mama, please," Mabel called after her. "Couldn't we manage one small girl? You didn't see that place. How miserable it was."

Nora stopped with her back to them. After a few moments she turned around. "You can be very persuasive, Mabel."

"Does that mean yes?" Mabel said.

"It means I will give it some serious consideration," Nora agreed.

Daisy winked at Mabel, and Mabel beamed back, thinking how happy poor little Ann would be if she didn't have to work in the orphanage laundry anymore.

Chapter Twenty-Three

. . . .

A Most

Distressing Event

DAISY GAVE MABEL A PIECE OF OLD ROPE AND A WET towel to take to school so she could string up a clothesline for her demonstration. Mabel put these things in a basket, along with her dryer spell and the bottles of extra wind. Miss Mantel would definitely be back at school today since the whole faculty was required to attend the competition.

"Do you have to take all of that with you?" Daisy said, watching Mabel carefully nestle the ten little bottles inside the basket. "What if you drop it? There'd be glass everywhere."

It wasn't broken glass Mabel worried about. It was

the powerful winds inside, which she had no idea how to release safely. "I need to return these bottles to Miss Mantel," Mabel said. "It's very important."

"And you can't do that tomorrow when you've got less to carry?"

"I really can't. But don't worry, Daisy, I'm not going to fly."

"Well, be careful," Daisy said, snatching a jug of cream off the table. "And don't forget your cat."

It took Mabel longer than usual to arrive at school because she walked so slowly. Preparations were already underway for the afternoon's event. Purple bunting had been hung from all the trees, and a large wooden podium, which Ruthersfield used for all their special events and award ceremonies, had been set up on the school grounds. The podium had rows of built-in chairs, and a purple and gold canvas roof, which, depending on the weather, provided shade for the faculty or protection from the rain.

"Get a move on, Mabel Ratcliff," Miss Reed said, as Mabel stood on the stairs, staring at the podium.

Mabel was imagining how it would feel to present her invention to all the teachers and important guests. She turned around and said, "Sorry, Miss Reed. I'm just so excited. And Angelina Tate will be here from the SOFTW!"

Miss Reed's face grew pinched, as if she had sucked on a lemon. "Enough of your chatter, Mabel Ratcliff." She pointed her wand at Mabel's chest, and two black *X*s flew out, attaching themselves to Mabel's lapel. "Two tardy demerits, girl. Now, get going, or you will be late for dance."

Mabel had hoped to drop the wind samples off with Miss Mantel before lessons started, but that would just have to wait until lunch. She couldn't afford another demerit for lateness, and there would be no time between dance class and sewing. Walking as fast as she dared, Mabel hurried along the corridor and up to the second floor. Lightning, who was exhausted from his long walk to school, waddled past her and kept on climbing. Off to the attic, Mabel guessed. This had become Lightning's favorite place to sleep during the day. A lot of his friends went up there. It was warm and sunny and kept a great many of the school cats out of the way when they weren't being used for flying lessons.

"Did you get your candle to work?" Mabel asked Ruby as the girls dusted off their wands at the end of sewing class. They were still making sweet dreams pillows filled with phoenix feathers, which had a tendency to stick to everything, and the ends of their wands were covered in the downy gold fluff that baby phoenixes shed when they grew their adult feathers.

"It's definitely better," Ruby replied. "Although the flame is really weak. I'm not sure it will burn forever, but Ma has had mine going all night and it's still no shorter."

"That's wonderful," Mabel whispered.

Miss Seymour clapped her hands. "Attention please, girls. Regular lessons are now over for today. After lunch we will all meet out on the lawn. I am sad that only a few students seem to be entering the competition. Perhaps the rest of you will be inspired when you see what your classmates have been up to."

"Did you cross-check all your ingredients, Mabel?" Ruby asked rather anxiously, sweeping up phoenix feathers. "Wind is so dangerous."

"Don't worry," Mabel reassured her. "I checked everything three times and practiced last night; the spell works beautifully." She gave a little shiver. "I do hope the judges like it. It's certainly going to make Daisy's life easier."

"Are you working with wind too?" Winifred said, startling the girls. It was disturbing the way she crept up on them. Her face was chalky white, and she had dark smudges under her eyes. "It's, it's difficult, isn't it? I've been staying up all night getting mine right." Raising her voice, Winifred added, "But my father is going to be so proud of me. He's going to love my invention. It's marvelous."

"No talking, please, girls. Finish clearing up," Miss Seymour said, and then with a smile at Winifred, "I'm glad you decided to enter the competition, Winifred. I'm sure your father will be delighted. It just goes to show what you can accomplish when you put your mind to something." Diana and Florence were giving Winifred puzzled looks as Mabel dragged Ruby off to a corner.

"What is she up to?" Mabel said. "Do you think she's making a dryer spell too? Has she stolen my idea? Look at her whispering with Diana and Florence. Even they seem mad at her. I bet she stole my idea. She's always hovering around us, listening in. I have to know what she's making."

"Calm down, Mabel," Ruby said. "Winifred is not an inventor."

"That's why I'm worried."

As soon as class ended, Mabel hurried over to Winifred, too anxious to wait for Ruby, who was helping Miss Seymour tidy up the bolts of fabric. "Are you really using wind in your invention?" Mabel said, unable to hid her concern.

"I am, Mabel, yes." Winifred started walking away, but Mabel followed her.

"What is it you're making, Winifred? I won't say, I promise. Please tell me."

"Well, I'm keeping it a secret from most people," Winifred said. "Except our maids. They've been helping me, actually. They love my invention. It's going to make their lives so much easier."

"Look, I'll tell you my idea if you tell me yours," Mabel said in a panic. She was desperate to know if Winifred had come up with a clothes dryer invention too.

Winifred hesitated. She glanced at Florence and Diana, who both shrugged nervously. "Very well," she agreed. "But not here. I'm not risking being overheard. And you can't say a word, Mabel."

"Of course I won't," Mabel said, clutching her basket but not moving.

Winifred started toward the door. "Are you coming then?" she hissed over her shoulder.

"I'd like to wait for Ruby." Mabel glanced at her friend, who was deep in conversation with Miss Seymour.

"Look, forget it, Mabel. I'm going to lunch." And nodding at Florence and Diana, Winifred marched out of the sewing room, her two friends scuttling behind.

"Wait," Mabel cried, hurrying after them. "Wait," she said again.

Winifred stopped and folded her arms. "So you've changed your mind?"

"Where are we going?" Mabel asked.

"You'll see," Winifred replied, and with her golden curls bouncing, she marched straight up to the third floor, stopping in front of the door to the attic. As usual, it was open a crack, so the cats could get in and out.

"Up there?" Mabel questioned, glancing around. Apart from the four girls, there was no one else in the corridor. "Why the attic?"

"This is where I've been working on my invention," Winifred whispered, pulling open the door.

"You're being ridiculous, Winifred. No one works in the attic."

"You get good, strong winds near the roof," Winifred said, ducking inside the stairway. Diana and Florence followed, but Mabel stood in the hallway, unsure what to do. "This was your idea," Winifred called back down. "You wanted to see what I was making, Mabel. So are you coming or not?"

Mabel hesitated a few seconds longer, her curiosity winning out. "I'm coming," she finally said, climbing the steep, narrow stairs to the attic. There was a ruffling of fur and a soft meowing as she stepped into the dusty space. Violet Featherstone's cat got up and stalked across the room, giving a yowl of displeasure at being disturbed. He yowled again and settled back down under the eaves.

"Winifred, are you sure about this?" Diana murmured.

"It was Mabel's idea, not mine," Winifred said. She fiddled with her necklace, a gold pendant that all the girls knew had belonged to her great-grandmother and had been a gift from the king of England. "And I'm not going to show you anything I've been up to, Mabel, until you show me yours," Winifred said. "How do I know I can trust you?"

"Of course you can trust me." Mabel sounded hurt.

"Let's just go," Florence broke in. "Please."

"You girls go if you like, but Mabel and I want to hear each other's ideas." Winifred nodded at Mabel. "Well, go on," she said. "You first."

And so, feeling more and more uneasy, but desperate to know what Winifred had been making, Mabel explained her invention.

"Gosh, that is so clever," Winifred gushed. "You could put up a little clothesline for a demonstration, couldn't you? But I bet you've already thought of that."

Mabel didn't answer. She could feel the sun against her cheek, streaming through the dusty windows, and she suddenly felt too warm, standing in the hot attic. "Your turn, Winifred," Mabel said.

"Well, you mustn't say a word," Winifred cautioned, "because mine really is top secret. Close your eyes," she ordered. "While I set it up."

"I'm not closing my eyes," Mabel said, realizing that this had been an extremely bad idea. "Show me now or I'm going." She began to walk toward the staircase, where Diana and Florence stood, hovering.

"Stop," Winifred ordered, holding out her hand. "I'm not going to show you, because you won't close your eyes, but I'll tell you, all right." Stepping toward Mabel, Winifred leaned in close, putting her mouth to Mabel's ear. "You're not going to believe this," she whispered, "but I'm making a clothes dryer too."

"You are?" There was a sharp pain in Mabel's foot as Winifred stamped on it.

"Ouch," Mabel yelped, and before she realized what was happening, she felt the basket being tugged out of her hand. "Hey!" Mabel yelled as Winifred raced across the attic. "Give that back. It's mine." Limping after the girls, Mabel clattered down the stairs and grabbed the door handle just as Winifred was pulling it shut. "No," Mabel screamed, holding on to the doorknob with both hands and leaning back to stop Winifred from closing it all the way. "Why are you doing this?" she sobbed.

"Because I need it more than you do, Mabel."

"But you have your own wind invention. That's what you told Miss Seymour."

"I wanted her to think that so she'll believe this is mine. And you'd never have come up here with me otherwise," Winifred panted, trying to tug the doorknob out of Mabel's hands. "You're so stupid, Mabel. I just parroted back what you said."

"Why?" Mabel said, starting to cry.

"Because I can't let my papa down, that's why." Winifred gritted her teeth as she pulled. "He is expecting me to make the Delacy family proud this afternoon. Papa thinks I've been working on my invention for weeks, and I will not disappoint him."

"You won't get away with this," Mabel sobbed. "Ruby will tell on you. She knows that's my spell." This startled Winifred, and she loosened her hold on the doorknob, long enough for Mabel to yank it toward her.

"Well, help me," Winifred snapped at Florence and Diana. "Otherwise we're all going to get in trouble." Putting their hands on top of Winifred's, the three girls pulled, and with a cry of frustration, Mabel felt the door move away from her and click shut. She tried turning the knob, but it wouldn't move. Mabel remembered that poor Violet Featherstone had gotten stuck in the attic last year. Sometimes a draft from the corridor window blew the door shut, and since it didn't open from the inside, you had to wait for someone to find you.

"You can't lock me in," she shouted. "They'll know who did it. I'll tell them everything."

"And who will believe you, over me?" Winifred said. "My father is Lord Winthrop Delacy. He's a good friend of Miss Brewers and he knows I never lie. You probably just came up here to find that stupid cat of yours, and the wind blew the door shut." Mabel could hear Winifred's raspy breathing, and the sound of glass bottles knocking against each other. There was an eerie silence, and then Winifred screamed, "I'm so tired of you showing me up, Mabel."

A sick queasiness rose in Mabel's throat. She leaned against the door, suddenly feeling faint. "Winifred, listen to me," Mabel said, her voice cracking with fear. "You mustn't open those bottles, only the one with a number three on it. That's the bottle with the spell inside. The rest are just wind samples, very powerful wind samples."

"I don't believe you for a minute, Mabel Ratcliff. Why would I open number three when you've drawn little stars around this one? Given it a ten out of ten? That's obviously your best spell."

"No, it's not," Mabel stressed. "The ten is for wind strength."

"I'm not stupid," Winifred said. "You just want to make me look bad."

Mabel heard the girls walking away. "Please don't leave me here," she begged.

Mabel pounded on the door a few more times, but everyone would be at lunch now. Sinking down on the bottom step, she hunched up her legs and wrapped her arms around them, salty tears slipping down her cheeks.

Chapter Twenty-Four

....

Things Get
Dramatically Worse

AFTER SITTING IN A DEJECTED HEAP FOR A WHILE, MABEL took off her glasses and rubbed at her eyes, streaking dirt across her face. There had to be another way out of here. She banged on the door until her fists ached, but no one was around to hear her. "I hate you, Winifred Delacy," Mabel said, speaking the words out loud. She knew Nora didn't like her to use the word "hate," but right at this moment it was the only possible way to describe her feelings toward Winifred. Trudging up the stairs, Mabel imagined all the things she would like to do to her. Cut off her fat golden ringlets, snip the feathers from her hat, push her into the canal.

The attic was stifling, and a wave of dizziness swept over Mabel. She sat down on a crate, dropping her head between her legs. Where were her smelling salts when she needed them? Mabel thought, feeling like Violet Featherstone, who always seemed to be about to faint.

When the attic door creaked open, Mabel jerked her head up, a wild hope surging through her. Maybe Winifred had changed her mind, or perhaps someone had noticed she was missing during lunch and had come up to try to find her. What she didn't expect to hear was Ruby shouting. "Hey, what are you doing? No! Let me out," followed by loud banging on the door. And then the sound of her calling rather frantically up the stairs, "Mabel, are you in here?"

"Ruby?" Mabel scrambled to her feet.

Footsteps pounded and Ruby exploded into the attic. "Winifred locked me in," Ruby fumed. "She said you were looking for me, and that I was to go straight to the attic, because it had something to do with your invention. So like a fool I raced up here, but as soon as I started climbing the stairs, Winifred shut the door on me." Ruby stamped her foot in frustration. "And it won't open from the inside because I've tried." Her voice shook with anger. "What on earth was I thinking? But I didn't know where you'd gone," Ruby reasoned.

"And you were talking to her at the end of class." She stared at Mabel. "Why did she shut us in?"

"Because she stole my invention," Mabel said, her lip quivering. "She made me think she had invented something too, and I wanted to see what it was, so she took me up here. I was scared she might have stolen my idea. I never expected her to steal my actual invention." Mabel watched the color literally drain from Ruby's face. She had pale skin to begin with, but it looked like someone had dipped her in a bucket of bleach. "And that's not the worst of it, Ruby," Mabel whispered. "She took all my wind samples too."

"What does that mean?" Ruby said, staring at Mabel.

"It means Winifred is about to unleash a wind that is so concentrated and strong it could . . ." Mabel paused a moment. "Well, I don't know how bad it will be because I never tested past a number five. That was powerful enough to tug laundry off a line, so imagine what a ten could do. Which is the bottle Winifred's planning to open. She thinks it's my best spell," Mabel explained. "And it's been sitting so long, it will be desperate to get out. Trapped wind is much more dangerous than I realized," Mabel admitted in a small voice. "You have to handle it very carefully."

✦✦✦

"This is bad," Ruby whispered, screwing up her face in anguish.

Mabel hurried over to one of the windows. She could see the podium down on the field where the teachers and guests were already starting to gather. Lord Winthrop Delacy sat next to Miss Brewer, wearing a gray top hat, and there was Angelina Tate from the Society of Forward-Thinking Witches, talking to Miss Seymour. The rest of the teachers were taking their seats, and a brass band had assembled in front of the school steps. Mabel could hear them playing a rousing rendition of the Ruthersfield song, "Spells of Glory." She watched as the girls filed out class by class, filling the chairs in front of the podium. Winifred walked demurely to her seat, giving a low curtsy to the podium before sitting down. She was holding a glass bottle in her hands, and Mabel gave a howl of frustration.

"We have to get out of here," Mabel said, pushing up the window. "Help," she yelled, waving madly. But the attic was too far away, and no one was looking up at the window to see them. Besides, the band played so loudly they would never be heard over the noise. "We'd break our necks if we jumped," Mabel said, looking at the ground.

"Can't you float down, Mabel? You said you floated as a baby."

"Not anymore. Not for years. And I'm certainly not going to risk it by throwing myself out an attic window."

"Wait a minute. Look over there," Ruby said.

Turning around, Mabel saw that Ruby was pointing at an open window on the far side of the attic. "It's still a thirty-foot drop, Ruby."

"Not down," Ruby said. "We go up, Mabel. See, the cats are getting in from somewhere." As she spoke, a black cat leaped through the window.

Mabel peered across the attic, slowly beginning to smile. "It might work, Ruby. You're a genius!" Picking her way over to the window, Mabel yanked it up as high as it would go and stuck her head out. There was a narrow ledge they could stand on, and craning her neck upward, Mabel saw that it was possible to climb right onto the roof from here. That way they could reach the iron drainpipe at the back of the building and climb down it to the ground.

"I'll go first," Mabel said, stepping out onto the ledge.

"Wait, Mabel," Ruby cried. "I'm not sure I can do this."

"Yes, you can. I'll help you." Holding on to the gutter, Mabel pulled herself up. "Don't look down," she panted, her hands growing sweaty as she grabbed at the slates. Kicking and scrabbling, Mabel managed to haul herself onto the roof, ripping her stockings in the process. She took a few deep breaths to steady her nerves. "All right, Ruby. I can pull you up now."

"Mabel, I'm really not sure I can do this," Ruby whimpered.

The band had stopped playing, but Mabel couldn't see across the roof from here, so she had no idea what was going on, until Miss Brewer's distinctive voice drifted toward them. It was impossible to hear exactly what the headmistress was saying, but Mabel caught the odd word or two. "Welcome," and "our honor," and "it's a pleasure to have you." Then the girls started clapping, and another woman, who Mabel guessed to be Angelina Tate, began addressing the crowd.

"Ruby, we have to hurry," Mabel said. "The girls are going to start demonstrating their inventions next, and I bet Winifred is one of the first."

"I'm scared of heights," Ruby whispered.

"Do you want to stay here and I'll go alone?" Mabel offered.

"No, I'm coming." Ruby slowly inched her way onto the ledge. "I can't let you do this by yourself." She gasped as a cat jumped out next to her, leaping onto the roof.

"Take my hand," Mabel said, reaching down. She grasped Ruby's fingers, which were damper than her own, and drawing on strength she didn't even know she had, Mabel yanked her friend toward her.

"These ridiculous petticoats," Ruby panted. "They just get in the way."

"Come on," Mabel said, scrambling up the gently sloping roof. At the top, she could see the assembly again. Cressida Williams in year three had stepped up to the front and appeared to be demonstrating a magic duster that was floating about the podium, brushing the guests' hats. Mabel could hear faint bursts of laughter. "Please, Ruby. We need to hurry." Ruby nodded but she didn't move. "You can do this. I know you can," Mabel encouraged her. "It's not that steep." Nodding again, Ruby slowly began to climb. As soon as she was near enough, Mabel leaned over and grabbed her hand. Holding tight to each other, the girls picked their way along the roof ridge and over to the heavy iron drainpipe that was fastened to a corner of the wall.

Looking down, Mabel saw that every few feet there was an iron band holding the drainpipe in place. "Right, Ruby. You're going to use the bands to place your feet on," Mabel said, reaching for the top of the pipe. "Just go slowly and follow me." She began to descend. Ruby was whimpering softly behind her, and Mabel prayed that they would make it in time. Halfway down there was a creaking sound. Mabel stopped climbing.

She held her breath. After a few moments, she moved again, more cautiously this time, her hands so slippery she found it difficult to hold on. As soon as her feet touched the ground, Mabel started to run, desperate to get to Winifred before she opened the bottle. There was another round of applause. As Mabel dashed across the grounds, she saw Winifred make her way to the front of the podium. She had strung a clothesline between two trees, and a frilly wet petticoat hung from it.

"I call my invention 'clothes dryer in a bottle,'" Winifred began, addressing the crowd in a loud, confident voice.

"No," Mabel yelled, charging over the grass. She lunged at Winifred, but Winifred dodged out of the way. Mabel lost her footing and fell. "Don't open it," Mabel gasped.

"Mabel Ratcliff," Miss Brewer roared. "How dare you disturb this event in such a manner, stampeding in here, covered in dirt. This is not how a Ruthersfield girl behaves." She banged her cane on the podium. "You should be ashamed of such behavior. Brawling like a fishwife."

Mabel scrambled to her feet. Her braids had come undone, but she didn't care. "Please, Miss Brewer. That is not Winifred's invention."

"Papa," Winifred broke in, "this is the girl who got

suspended. The one the Cranfords were telling us about."

Lord Winthrop Delacy rose from his seat and pointed a finger at Mabel. His face boiled with heat and his hand shook. "That child should be expelled. Accusing my daughter . . ."

"You will go straight to my office," Miss Brewer said, with another bang of her cane. "Now."

Miss Reed, the flying teacher, marched down from the podium and took Mabel's arm in a vicelike grip. "I will accompany the child."

"Thank you, Miss Reed." Miss Brewer turned back to Winifred. "Please continue, Winifred."

"No," Mabel screamed. "It's the wrong bottle, Winifred. Don't open it."

"Wait!" Miss Seymour jumped up. But it was too late. Winifred was pulling out the cork.

With a loud whooshing sound, a black funnel-shaped tornado spun out of the bottle. Mabel stumbled backward, knocked over by the force of the wind. It howled in fury, tearing the clothesline from the tree and spinning straight at the podium. There was a gasp from the assembled girls as they watched the tornado swoop under the canvas roof and pick up the whole structure, lifting the entire Ruthersfield faculty and all the guests into the air. It spun the podium in wild circles. Top hats, canes, and glasses came pouring down, followed by a shower of knitted wand cases, the wands scattering all over the grass. Trapped in their seats, the teachers and guests held on tight. One minute they were sitting there in a mass of purple gowns and finery, the next they were all gone. Every single one of them. Except for Miss Reed, who had let go of Mabel and was waving her smelling salts in front of her face, blubbering out a stream of nonsense. In numb shock, Mabel watched the podium hurtle across the sky. The wind taking it away had come from the coast, and that was probably where it was heading, Mabel guessed. Back out to sea.

Chapter Twenty-Five

·····································

The Chase

A NUMBER OF THE GIRLS HAD FAINTED, FALLING gracefully to the ground one after another. Florence had been the first, setting off a chain reaction of collapsing students. Miss Reed wrung her hands, looking around in distress, as if searching for someone to tell her what to do. "All the teachers," she kept mumbling. "Every last one of them. And Lord Winthrop Delacy as well."

"Miss Reed, shouldn't we go after them?" Mabel said. "Before it's too late."

"Yes, yes, of course," Miss Reed whispered, not making any move to go.

Taking the initiative, Mabel ran to the shed and grabbed an armful of broomsticks. She raced back and tossed one to the flying teacher, throwing the rest on the ground. "We can't waste time. We have to go now," she shouted. "Please, everybody, grab a broom."

"But what can we do?" Violet Featherstone cried. "There's no way to stop them. They'll end up getting swept out to sea and drowned." A great wail of despair went up from the girls at this, and the air was thick with the scent of smelling salts.

"Where's my cat?" Miss Reed moaned, perching sideways on her broomstick. "Kittypuss, Kittypuss, here, pretty kitty," she called in a thin, quivery voice.

"No time for cats," Mabel yelled, hitching up her petticoats and flinging one leg over her broomstick. "Who's coming with me?" There was no answer from the girls, just the sound of hysterical sobbing.

"Where's my papa?" Winifred wailed. "What have you done with him, Mabel?"

"Get a broom and let's go," Mabel ordered, whereupon Winifred collapsed on the grass in a faint.

Ruby was calling for her cat, but Mabel shook her head. "No, Ruby. Leave him. Ride like this; it's much faster."

Copying Mabel, Ruby lifted her petticoats as she swung her leg over. "My mother would be horrified, seeing me fly this way," Ruby said, swooping into the air.

"She'll be even more horrified if she hears we've lost the entire staff of Ruthersfield, including Lord Winthrop Delacy and the mayor."

"Oh, Mabel, too high," Ruby gasped, following Mabel up past the trees. "We're not supposed to fly this high, and I really do have a fear of heights."

"Forget the rules. Just don't look down," Mabel said. And aiming west, she sped off toward the coast, hunched low over the handle for a more streamlined ride.

There was no sign of the teachers, and Mabel scanned the sky, worrying about what would happen if they were never found. The school would have to close down while the board of governors replaced them all and found a new headmistress. Except that wouldn't work, Mabel realized, because most of the board of governors had been swept away too. This was a catastrophe of the highest order. Mabel groaned, terrified that they wouldn't be able to stop the teachers from blowing all the way over to Greenland, which seemed to be the direction they were heading in.

"I smell salt," Ruby shouted. "We must be near the coast."

There was a definite saline tang to the air, and glancing down, Mabel saw the Melton Bay pier. Mr.

Miller's donkeys had escaped again and were running along the sand, and Mabel wondered if the sight of a flying pavilion had scared them.

"There they are," Ruby suddenly screamed. "By the cliffs."

Far down the beach, the jagged white rocks rose out of the sea, signaling danger to ships and swimmers. Huge breakers crashed against them, and gusting over the top of the cliffs was the pavilion, which looked more like a fast-moving thundercloud. It was dark and purple, as if brewing an enormous storm, except Mabel knew it wasn't rain that would come pouring down on the ocean, but a tempest of tumbling witches.

"Do you have your wand with you, Ruby?" Mabel shouted. "I've lost mine." The wind took her words and tossed them away, and Mabel had to repeat herself three times before Ruby heard.

"Yes, I do," Ruby yelled back, and Mabel nodded. There was a spell they had learned last term called the Stop It Now Spell. It was meant to halt fast-moving objects and was the only thing Mabel could think of that just might work. They had gone outside and practiced it on hares, which always seemed plentiful in the meadows around Potts Bottom. Mabel had had no difficulty with the spell, and it had been great fun making the hare stop and start as it hopped across the field. But casting it while flying was another matter entirely, because you needed an extremely steady hand.

She flew as close to Ruby as she dared. Mabel didn't want to get too close, because if she lost control of her broomstick (which was entirely possible at the speed they were flying), they would crash into each other. And neither of the girls could swim.

"Get ready," Mabel yelled, slowing down slightly for the transfer. With a great deal of wobbling, Ruby managed to get the wand out of her pocket, and Mabel reached across with one hand, feeling for the first time like this whole awful matter might not end in disaster. As the girls leaned toward each other, a sharp gust of wind knocked against them. Before Mabel could get a good grip on the wand, Ruby grabbed for her broomstick to steady herself, and they both let out a howl as the wand slipped through Mabel's fingers and plummeted toward the water.

"Oh, blast it all," Mabel swore, diving after the wand as fast as she could. But she wasn't quick enough, and with a cry of despair, Mabel watched it hit the waves and sink out of sight.

The girls stared at the water, waiting for Ruby's wand to reappear, bounce back up, but of course it wouldn't. Even though their school wands were made of black walnut wood, the handles were weighted with unicorn hoof. This helped ground their spells and give them stability, but it also meant that the wands didn't float.

"Now what?" Ruby said, starting to cry.

"I don't know," Mabel croaked. She thought of all those strong Ratcliff women her mother had told her about. They wouldn't give up so easily. "Come on, Ruby. We have to keep flying. We can't lose sight of them, otherwise we may never find them again."

"I'm so tired," Ruby sobbed, but she flew on beside Mabel. "Are you sure you don't have your wand, Mabel?"

Mabel had checked in her pocket at least six times, but she checked again, because she couldn't believe it wasn't there. It must have fallen out on the roof.

"Empty," Mabel shouted, shaking her head. There was nothing in her pinafore pocket except a sticky mess of cobweb stuck to the lining. She had forgotten all about her cobweb experiment, and wondered if the growing powder had worked on it. Well, they had nothing else to try. It was worth a go. "Ruby, I need your help," Mabel yelled, peeling the web free. "You've got to stop crying and concentrate. I have a plan, but I can't do it alone." Ruby nodded, tilting her head down quickly and wiping her eyes on her shoulder. "We're going to use this cobweb as a net," Mabel said. "If we can fly in front of the podium, we'll stretch this out between us and trap them in it." Mabel panted for breath. Talking and flying at the same time was difficult. "Once their momentum has been stopped, the wind will die down and we can tug them back to shore."

"It's a cobweb," Ruby yelled. "This will never work."

"We don't have another choice." Mabel held out her hand. "Take a corner, Ruby, and do not let go."

"Won't it rip?" Ruby said, doing exactly what Mabel told her.

"I hope not," Mabel shouted. "I've been experimenting with it."

The girls slowly flew apart, and Mabel gave a satisfied cry as the cobweb started stretching. It did seem unbelievably strong, with the texture of India rubber, which must have something to do with the lion breath she had added to her strengthening potion, and the growing powder had clearly worked. The cobweb stretched across the sky, as if a giant spider had spun it.

"Now go as fast as you can," Mabel panted. "We have to get in front of them."

After fifteen minutes of flying, they were gaining slowly on the whirlwind of teachers, but Mabel had never been so tired, and she was nervous Ruby might fall off her broomstick from exhaustion. "Come on,"

Mabel encouraged. "We can do this, Ruby."

Ruby had started to cry again, tears slipping down her cheeks and falling into the ocean. The girls refused to give up though, using every last ounce of strength as they sped toward the purple mass.

"We're close," Mabel yelled. "Keep going, Ruby." And then the wind turned, swirling fiercely to the left, and tipping the podium upside down. Mabel watched in horror as the witches started falling from the sky, skirts blowing up like inside-out umbrellas. "Angle your broomstick and dive, Ruby," Mabel shouted, her throat raw from screaming. "Now spread apart," she ordered. "Swoop down underneath them." The cobweb widened but it didn't break, and Mabel prayed that the strands would hold. "Brace yourself," she yelled, as the crowd of witches and dignitaries hurtled into it, trapped like a catch of giant purple fish.

Mabel's arms burned with pain, and Ruby screamed. But neither of the girls let go. The cobweb stretched and stretched, tugging them backward and breaking the momentum of the fall. Glancing down, Mabel saw the teachers flapping about, expressions of shock on all their faces. Miss Brewer's hair puffed out in a frizzy gray cloud. Her bloomers were showing and her mouth kept opening and closing like a salmon just pulled from the water. Lord Delacy had lost his hat, and he appeared to be sucking his thumb. Mabel couldn't speak. She was crying so hard her glasses had misted up, and when she smiled at Ruby, it was through a blur of happy tears.

Chapter Twenty-Six

••••••••••••••••••••••••••••••••

Well Done, Mabel Ratcliff

TUGGING THE NET OF WITCHES BACK TO RUTHERSFIELD was a slow, grueling business, but Mabel and Ruby laughed the whole way, pushed on by the adrenaline of success. As they flew over Melton Bay, they saw Miss Reed heading sedately toward them with Kittypuss.

"You're a little late," Miss Brewer snapped from inside the cobweb as Miss Reed hovered beside them. "Mabel saved the day."

"So did Ruby," Mabel called back. "I couldn't have done it without her."

"Such an undignified way to be rescued," Miss Reed

murmured, noting the jumble of witches. Most of their hair had come unpinned, and they resembled a net of mermaids, rather than respectable teachers.

Mabel waved at some children on the beach, who were jumping and pointing, staring up at the witches as they flew across the sky. A great sense of pride and achievement swelled in Mabel's chest, and she couldn't stop smiling.

Word had traveled fast, as was usually the case in Potts Bottom. A number of sobbing girls had stumbled into town with horrifying tales of what had happened. So when Mabel and Ruby finally landed outside the school, a large crowd of villagers was gathered there to greet them. Mabel rolled off her broomstick and lay on her back for a moment, listening to the crowd cheer. As she got slowly to her feet, the roar from the crowd intensified. Mrs. Tanner swept Ruby into her arms, and Nora rushed over to Mabel, wrapping her in a tight hug and kissing the top of her head.

"I came down here as soon as Daisy told me what was happening. She had just come out of the baker's and saw the podium fly off. I was terrified you wouldn't come back," Nora whispered. "I was so scared I might lose you."

"I was quite scared myself," Mabel admitted. Every

muscle in her body ached, and her palms were raw with blisters.

Miss Brewer slowly stood up, helped by Miss Seymour and Angelina Tate. The headmistress attempted to pin her hair back into place with shaking fingers. She walked over to Mabel and Ruby and lowered her head. The crowd fell silent, and after a moment Miss Brewer raised her eyes. "Mabel Ratcliff and Ruby Tanner," she said, in a voice full of reverence. "What you did today took an unbelievable amount of courage, quick thinking, and determination. You showed the world what a true Ruthersfield girl is capable of, and I applaud you both from the bottom of my heart." There was a great deal of cheering at this, and Miss Brewer had to hold up her hand for silence. "You displayed strength of character and true spirit, and some day, girls, I believe either one of you will make a head girl that Ruthersfield can be proud of, the sort of head girl who will be remembered for generations to come."

Mabel stood beside Nora, too tired to speak, thinking that perhaps Mabel wasn't such a bad name to have after all.

"I would also like to announce," Miss Brewer continued, bestowing a smile on Mabel, "that it is time we changed our flying requirements here at Ruthersfield. From now on girls will learn to ride their broomsticks bicycle style and the use of cats will be optional."

"Yes!" Mabel cried, hugging Ruby, who was standing beside her.

"May I ask that you reconsider?" Miss Reed interjected. "Such a practice is not for young ladies."

"Miss Reed, after the show of heroics we have all just witnessed, I'm surprised at you. Ruthersfield is moving into the twentieth century, and I suggest that you join us there. As for you," Miss Brewer said, turning to Winifred, who was sobbing in her father's arms. "You are no longer welcome at this school. I am expelling you, Winifred Delacy." A gasp rippled its way around the girls. "What you did was despicable. Stealing is not to be tolerated. But on a far more serious note, your actions today could have taken many lives. If it hadn't been for Mabel Ratcliff's and Ruby Tanner's show of bravery, you would probably have ended up in Scrubs Prison." The gasp became a crazy chattering of voices. Everyone knew that Scrubs was a high security prison for witches, and once inside, a witch was never released.

"I'm sorry," Winifred sobbed. "I just wanted my father to be proud of me. Please let me stay."

"There is no discussion here, Winifred. You will leave the property at once."

Mabel couldn't help but feel sorry for Lord Winthrop Delacy. He was looking at his daughter with such sadness and disappointment, and Mabel knew the Delacys' lives would never be the same again.

Police Constable Lambert from the Potts Bottom force stepped forward and tipped his hat at Lord Winthrop. "Your Lordship, I must ask that your daughter hand over her wand immediately. Under Yorkshire law she is banned from practicing magic ever again."

"But I want to be a crystal ball gazer for the queen," Winifred sobbed.

Lord Delacy bowed his head in shame, and Mabel noticed that he had a bald spot right at the back. Without his top hat it was rather noticeable, and he kept brushing his hand across it, as if trying to conceal the patch of pink, slightly sunburned skin. Now that the competition was over, Mabel decided that she would go back to working on a hair-growing potion that not only made hair thicker and longer but could also be a cure for baldness. There was clearly a need for such a potion, and she gave an enormous yawn, wondering if mermaid hair might work well as an active ingredient. Mermaids were known for their thick, beautiful, quick-growing hair, so it seemed like a good place to start.

"Mabel?" Miss Brewer was saying, interrupting her thoughts.

"I'm sorry, Miss Brewer, could you repeat that?" Mabel said, smothering another yawn.

"I said that since you didn't get a chance to present your invention to the committee, along with most of the other girls entering, we will reschedule the assembly for next week."

Angelina Tate stepped over, still looking a little windswept. "I would just like to say a big thank you from the Society of Forward-Thinking Witches to both of you girls. What you did today showed creativity and genius, and it would be my great pleasure to make you honorary members of the society. Mabel Ratcliff and Ruby Tanner, you are the sort of young witches that will lead our community into the new century. That cobweb net you came up with . . ." Angelina Tate shook her head and looked over at Miss Seymour. "Genius, really genius."

Mabel gave an embarrassed shrug. "I was just playing around with ideas," she said. "It was an experiment. I didn't really know what I was inventing."

"That's how some of our greatest new inventions are discovered," Miss Seymour pointed out. "By accident."

"Mabel, Ruby," the girls started chanting. They were clapping and stamping their feet. Miss Brewer didn't tell them to quiet down, because after such an eventful afternoon, some clapping and stamping seemed entirely appropriate.

Chapter Twenty-Seven

....

A Girl of the Twentieth Century!

DAISY HAD NEVER BEEN SO PROUD. SHE CLUCKED around the kitchen like a mother hen, filling the big tin bathtub with hot water and washing Mabel clean. Afterward, Mabel put on her trousers, because she couldn't bear the thought of getting back into petticoats and a frock, and sat down at the table to consume a large plate of ham and cucumber sandwiches, two currant buns, a slice of ginger cake, and a bowl of raspberries, picked fresh from the garden by Nora.

Lightning seemed to sense that his services weren't going to be needed anymore, because he sat close beside Mabel's chair, looking up at her out of big worried eyes.

"He's nervous he might lose his supply of kippers and cream," Mabel said, scratching Lightning behind the ears.

"Which he steals most of, I would like to point out," Daisy added. "Good riddance to him, if you ask me."

"Oh, Daisy, you don't mean that." Mabel patted Lightning's fur, sending a cloud of black hairs into the air. "I know you would miss him dreadfully."

"Ummph," Daisy muttered. "Why don't you invent an easy way to pick up pet fur? Then I might feel more warmly toward him."

"Interesting idea," Mabel said. "I'll add that to my list of things to work on."

Mabel was just finishing the last currant bun when a photographer from the *Potts Bottom Gazette* arrived, asking to take her picture. "Would you like to change into something smarter for the photograph?" he suggested, eyeing Mabel's trousers with distaste. "A pretty dress, perhaps?"

"No, thank you," Mabel replied. "But could we take the picture outside?" Leading him into the garden, she stood beneath the apple tree and, clutching her broomstick, smiled proudly at the camera.

The next morning when Mabel got to school, Miss Seymour came hurrying over, waving a copy of the *Gazette*. And there, on the ladies home page, were two photographs, one of Mabel and one of Ruby. Underneath, in bold letters, it said, DARE TO PUSH BOUNDARIES AND FLY AGAINST THE WIND. ELEVEN-YEAR-OLDS MABEL RATCLIFF AND RUBY TANNER SHOW US HOW IT'S DONE.

"Of course they should have put you both on the front page with the real news," Miss Seymour remarked. But she was smiling. "Not with the recipes and fashion tips."

"I don't mind. And at least I got to wear my trousers in the picture," Mabel said. "I'm thinking of making Miss Brewer a pair for Christmas," she added. "When she sees how comfortable they are, maybe she'll change her mind and let me wear them to school."

The headmistress had kept her word about altering broomstick-riding protocol, but she refused to let the girls wear trousers. "This is a school for young ladies," Miss Brewer had told Mabel firmly. "You make some excellent points about safety and control, Mabel, but we will not be resorting to totally heathen ways."

The following week, when Mabel finally demonstrated her clothes dryer in a bottle (her basket having been discovered in the rhododendron bushes by the school gardener), she won first place and the patent to put it into production. "A fun and useful invention that will make life a lot easier for a great many households," Angelina Tate had said.

However Miss Brewer did give Mabel a firm talking to about harvesting wind, saying, "It is far more dangerous than playing with fire, Mabel Ratcliff, and you are to ask assistance before working with the elements again."

"Yes, Miss Brewer," Mabel replied. She handed over the remains of her wind specimens to Miss Mantel, who uncorked them in the potions room, making sure there was plenty of polar bear breath on hand to freeze the more powerful winds as they came out.

The competition judges had been most impressed by Ruby's everlasting candle, although she couldn't seem to get it to burn for longer than four months. It was Mabel who finally worked out that the addition of phoenix blood would keep the candle burning indefinitely.

Florence and Diana were given a wand whipping from Miss Brewer when their part in locking Mabel and Ruby in the attic came to light. They were both put on cobweb duty for a month and went around with tearstained faces, mumbling "sorry" to Mabel every time they saw her in the hallways.

As for Winifred Delacy... Well, her parents employed a governess who had answered their advertisement in the *Ladies' Home Journal*, requesting someone who would provide a strict, firm hand for their daughter.

And it was quite a surprise to Mabel the first time she saw Nanny Grimshaw marching Winifred around Potts Bottom, a look of smug satisfaction on her sour face. Whatever Winifred had done, no one deserved the torture of Nanny Grimshaw, and Mabel couldn't help feeling rather sorry for her former classmate. She even considered slipping Winifred a little cat-calming brew to put in Nanny's tea. Whenever the girls passed each other, Winifred would look away or pretend to examine a wildflower, but she did occasionally give a small nod to show she had heard Mabel say hello. Since she couldn't wear her witch's hat anymore, she had taken to wearing elaborate feather-trimmed bonnets that looked like she had a bird nesting on her head.

One warm July morning, a few weeks before the summer holidays, Nora surprised Mabel with a visit to the orphanage. Even though Mabel wished they could have brought home all the children, she was delighted when little Ann came back to live with them. Daisy made up a bed in the corner of Mabel's room, and whenever Ann woke with bad dreams in the night, Mabel would put on a puppet show with her teddy bear and stuffed donkey, making them dance around the room. Nora added Ann's name to the family tree, and before long none of them could remember what life had been like without her.

★★★

As the years went by, Mabel continued to push boundaries, suggesting that the school start up Ruthersfield's first broomstick gymnastics team. She pointed out that it would provide exercise and sportsmanship for the girls, as well as coordination, balance, and confidence. Finally, in year ten, Miss Brewer agreed, and their new flying instructor (who had taken over from Miss Reed) was most enthusiastic, being a member of the SOFTW and open to new ideas.

Science became part of the Ruthersfield curriculum, and it was (to no one's great surprise) Mabel's favorite subject. She spent hours in the potions lab experimenting with new ideas, still trying to come up with a hair-restoring tonic, and wanting to know what would happen if you added powdered dragon scales to a basic courage potion or stirred worm wind into an invisibility spell. Some of her creations were successful and some were complete disasters. Like the time Mabel's cauldron exploded, spewing a fast-forward spell everywhere, because she had wanted to see what would happen if you added leopard spots to the mixture. Not a good idea, Mabel discovered.

In year twelve, Ruby Tanner was made deputy head girl, and with a great deal of pride, Mabel Ratcliff accepted the position of head girl. She was, in everyone's opinion, the best head girl Ruthersfield had ever had, expanding the good works program to include a twice yearly day out at the seaside for the orphanage children, and a weekly story-time and cake hour. Mabel would bring along a cake donated by the Potts Bottom Bakery and read to the children from one of the books in Nora's library. Inspired by the stew pot, she also invented a magic picnic hamper for the orphanage. It was the size of a small basket and provided a full teatime spread for sixty children, complete with sandwiches, cakes, buns, and lemonade. Like the stew pot, the picnic hamper always contained a lovely element of surprise, except when fish paste sandwiches showed up, which all the children hated.

Mabel Ratcliff was one of the first Ruthersfield girls to study magical science at university. She moved to London in 1908, and over the course of her life invented many wonderful things. Mabel did finally come up with a hair-growing potion, but it took her years before she figured out that powdered snakeskin had miraculous regrowth properties and was the answer she had been looking for. Mixed with mermaid hair and rainbow dust, it made a fabulous hair-restoring cream that came in a wide variety of colors, and for Daisy's sixty-fifth birthday Mabel presented her with a bottle. Much to Daisy's great delight, she instantly grew a mane of thick red curls, just like Nellie Glitters's!

Mabel's greatest achievement though (and the one she was proudest of) was when she accomplished her dream of harnessing star power. It became the cleanest, most efficient form of energy available. And in 1929, Mabel Ratcliff helped design the first rocket broomstick to travel to the moon. But, however impressive these inventions were, it was always her hair potion that she was best remembered for.

Having no plans to marry, Mabel was taken quite off guard when at thirty-five years old she met and fell in love with William Sanders, a landscape artist who also pushed boundaries. He took the Ratcliff surname, giving up his own, and it was William, not Mabel, who stayed home with their only child, a baby girl they christened Magnolia. William Ratcliff made an excellent househusband, raising many eyebrows when he took little Magnolia to the park. She showed a great deal of talent for hanging upside down from trees, but not the slightest hint of magic. Mabel was a touch disappointed when it became clear that Magnolia had not inherited her magical gene, but she never gave up hoping that one of her grandchildren or great-grandchildren might someday get the gift.

As for Nora Ratcliff . . . Well, she stayed in Potts Bottom for the rest of her life, becoming head of the Rose Growers' Association and dying in bed at the grand old age of eighty-five. Little Ann grew up to become a schoolteacher, and since both she and Mabel lived in London, they gave the cottage and most of the furniture to Daisy, who had served Nora faithfully since she was sixteen. There were a few books and possessions the girls wanted to keep, but the most important thing Mabel took with her, and eventually passed along to her own daughter, was the Ratcliff family tree.

Every once in a while on hot summer days, when a longing would swell up inside Mabel, a longing for the mother she would never know, she liked to spread out her family tree on the kitchen table, tracing the Ratcliffs right back to the thirteenth century. She always remembered what Nora had told her. If a sapling is moved to a new home, given the right care and love, it will set down fresh roots and flourish. Mabel was extremely proud of her Ratcliff heritage. But she never forgot her humble beginnings either. In fact, not long after moving to London, she purchased two large terra-cotta flowerpots, which she placed on each side of her front door. And every summer, as soon as the weather turned warm, she would fill them with Royal Duchess roses and ornamental ferns, in private memory of both her mothers.

A Taste of Life
in the 1890s

TO EXPERIENCE WHAT LIFE MIGHT HAVE BEEN LIKE FOR Mabel growing up in Victorian times, try out some of these recipes and ideas. Ask an adult for permission and/or to help you set up and use kitchen equipment, crack eggs, cut with knives, or take pans in and out of the oven, etc.

Calming Peppermint Tea

This is what Nanny Grimshaw tells Daisy to make for her when she has one of her headaches coming on. Nanny likes to take a cup up to her bedroom and insists on not being disturbed. Peppermint tea is extremely good for relieving head pain, and Mabel always loves it when she sees Daisy gathering mint from the garden, because she knows it probably means Nanny Grimshaw won't be bothering her for a couple of hours!

~ INGREDIENTS ~

1 handful fresh mint leaves
2 cups of boiling water
Honey to taste

~ METHOD ~

Wash the mint leaves and put them in a teapot. Pour in boiling water and let steep for 5 minutes. Strain. Pour out and enjoy with a little honey stirred in to sweeten.

Nighttime Treacle Posset

This is a lovely, warm, milky drink that Nora sometimes brings up to Mabel right before bed. It is perfect sipped between flannel sheets while listening to a bedtime story.

Serves 3 tired children.

~ INGREDIENTS ~

. . . .

2½ cups of whole milk

4 tablespoons of treacle (molasses)

~ METHOD ~

. . . .

Whisk together the milk and the treacle in a saucepan and heat until warm. Pour into your favorite bedtime mug and enjoy. Sweet, warm, and comforting.

Crystallized Flowers

Daisy makes these beautiful candied flowers to decorate cakes and special-occasion desserts. Her favorite flowers to use are violets, pansies, crab apple blossoms, and rose petals. After being coated with superfine sugar and left to dry, they get crisp, sparkly, and delicious.

~ INGREDIENTS ~

Pesticide-free edible flowers

Pasteurized powdered egg white or meringue powder
   (available from cake-decorating stores)

Superfine sugar (It works well if you have an empty salt
   shaker to put the sugar into.)

~ METHOD ~

1. Brush the dirt off the flowers but don't wash them.

2. Cover a cookie sheet or tray in wax paper.

3. Dilute the powdered egg white or meringue powder with
    a little water.

4. Hold the flower in your fingers or use a pair of tweezers

and dip into the liquid to cover the flower, leaf, and stem completely.

5. Sprinkle on a coat of sugar. Shake gently to release excess sugar.

6. Lay the flowers on the cookie sheet, making sure they don't touch.

7. Let dry in a cool place for 2 to 4 hours.

8. Use to decorate cakes and puddings or any special-occasion dessert. Sprinkle on ice cream for a pretty and unusual crunch, or just eat the flowers on their own, like candy!

9. These crystallized flowers keep well. You can store them in an airtight container, layered between sheets of tissue paper, for up to one month. Flowers can also be stored in the freezer for six months.

Perfect Cucumber Sandwiches

Nora and Mabel adore these delicate tea sandwiches of Daisy's. Wafer-thin rounds of cucumber layered between thin slices of buttered white (traditional) or wheat (if you prefer—but Daisy would never use) bread. It is important to cut the crusts off and arrange in dainty triangles (rectangles are also acceptable) on a pretty plate.

~ INGREDIENTS ~

½ English cucumber, peeled

Good butter at room temperature

6 slices of best quality white bread

Salt and white pepper

~ METHOD ~

1. Slice the cucumbers as thinly as you can. Lay them on a paper towel and put another paper towel on top. Gently pat to absorb some of the moisture.

2. Spread each slice of bread generously with butter.

3. Arrange the cucumbers on half the slices, overlapping

each round, and sprinkle with salt and pepper.

4. Top with the remaining bread slices.

5. Press down firmly and cut off the crusts, and then cut into neat triangles or rectangles. Try to make the sandwiches the same size.

6. Serve immediately with a nice cup of tea.

Daisy's Teatime Seedcake

Daisy often makes this cake for tea. It is simple and delicious—a good, plain cake that won't spoil Mabel's appetite for her supper! Be careful with the caraway seeds though, because their flavor is strong and a little goes a long way. One time, Mabel decided to experiment and put in ten tablespoons, and the results were so nasty even Lightning turned his nose up at it!

~ INGREDIENTS ~

1 stick softened salted butter

½ cup sugar

2 large eggs

¼ cup almond flour (finely ground almonds)

1⅛ cups self-rising flour

1 to 2 teaspoons of caraway seeds—depending on how strong
    a flavor you want

2 to 3 tablespoons milk

1 tablespoon raw sugar (sometimes called turbinado) for
    sprinkling on top

~ Method ~

· ·

1. Preheat the oven to 350 degrees F.

2. Grease a 7- or 8-inch cake pan or an 8-x-4-inch loaf pan.

3. Cream the butter and sugar together until light and fluffy, and then beat in the eggs one at a time.

4. Using a metal spoon, carefully fold in the almond flour, self-rising flour, and caraway seeds.

5. Add the milk one tablespoon at a time until the mixture softens, and then spoon into the prepared pan.

6. Bake in the center of the oven for about 45 minutes. The cake is ready when a sharp knife inserted into the middle comes out clean.

7. Cool on a wire rack for ten minutes before removing from pan. Sprinkle with raw sugar.

8. Slice and enjoy with a nice cup of tea.

Nora's Rose Petal Potpourri

This pretty potpourri of rose petals will add a delicate, floral ambience to your home, a must for any hostess. Display it in a glass dish and let the lovely lingering scent welcome guests when they stop by for tea.

~ Supplies ~

One dozen roses—the more fragrant the better (Nora always used her Royal Duchesses.)

A cookie tray

Newspaper

½ teaspoon ground cinnamon

½ teaspoon dried lavender

Rose essential oil or rose water (optional)

Sealable glass container

~ Method ~

1. Remove the petals from the flowers and spread them over the cookie tray. Cover with a layer of newspaper.

2. Once the petals start to get a little dry and crispy around the edges, place in a sealable glass jar. Add the cinnamon and lavender, and if your roses are not as powerful as Nora's, sprinkle over a few drops of rose oil or rose water to deepen the scent.

3. Close the container and shake. Place in a warm, dry spot and leave for about 24 hours. Shake again.

4. Pour into a pretty glass dish and breathe deeply!

Lavender Wands

Daisy makes these lavender wands every year when the lavender is in bloom. She tucks them into Nora's and Mabel's clothes drawers to scent their undergarments. Nanny Grimshaw insists on keeping a lavender wand close at hand, so she can wave it under her nose any time she smells an unpleasant odor!

These may sound a little fussy to make, but they are really quite simple if you follow the directions carefully. Read through first before starting to make your wand.

~ Method ~

. . . .

1. Begin by gathering a bunch of lavender (between 20 and 30 stems is a good number), keeping the flower stalks long—about twice as long as the buds of the flower. If you plan to weave ribbon around your wand at the end, use an odd number of stalks.
2. Strip off any leaves remaining on the flower stalks.
3. Bundle the bunch up and, using a rubber band or piece of string, tie the bundle together right below the flowers. If you like you can tie a narrow (⅛-inch) ribbon around that.

4. Holding the bouquet with the flowers pointing down, fold the long stalks around the flowers, enclosing them in a narrow, cagelike structure. The stalks should surround the flower buds like a birdcage. Some of the stalks may split a little (that's okay!), but if you work quickly while the stalks are still fresh, it is easier.

5. Evenly space your stalks and secure underneath the tips of the flowers with another rubber band. If you like you can take a piece of ribbon and weave it over and under the stalks of the cage, going around and around to make a pretty pattern.

6. Keep a wand handy to wave under your nose, or tuck one into your clothes drawer.

Personalized Smelling Salts

Mabel never remembers to carry her smelling salts, but the Ruthersfield girls always have little bags of smelling salts tucked away in their pockets. To make some of your own, simply mix up a batch of aromatic salts, personalizing them with different scents to suit your mood. Choose rosemary and peppermint if you need an energizing lift, or lavender when you want to be soothed. Spoon them into a pretty cloth bag and sniff whenever you're tired or in need of a boost.

~ INGREDIENTS ~

. . . .

¼ cup Epsom salts (available at most pharmacies)

3 drops of your favorite essential oil, or any combination of essential oils (available from health food stores and craft shops)

~ METHOD ~

. . . .

1. Put the Epsom salts into a small bowl. Add essential oil and mix. Pour into a little potpourri bag and tuck discreetly away in your pocket.

2. You can mix different oils together, so have fun experimenting—just keep to 3 drops per ¼ cup. Below is a list of oils to help you decide which ones you want to use.

Lavender—calming, relaxing

Rosemary—energizing

Peppermint—energizing, refreshing

Chamomile—relaxing, calming

Rose—centering

Vanilla—warm, sunny, calming

Acknowledgments

HUGE THANKS TO MY FABULOUS AGENT, ANN TOBIAS, for helping me dig out Mabel's story from an extremely rough first draft and then working with me through countless rounds of revision. You are the best!

Thanks to my wonderful editor, Paula Wiseman, and everyone at Paula Wiseman Books, for taking such good care of Mabel and giving her a marvelous home!

I am so grateful to Sebastien Mesnard, for his gorgeous artwork, and to Chloë Foglia, for designing the perfect cover.

Thank you to Jane Gilbert Keith, for reading draft after draft of *Mabel*, offering your thoughts, listening to me chatter on, and never once complaining.

A special thank-you to Ann Gilbert, for sharing her wisdom and experiences with me on the subject of adoption. Your insights and comments were invaluable, and *Mabel* is a better book because of them.

I would never have written Mabel's story if my nephew Max hadn't leaned across the dinner table one day and said, "I think you should write Great-Granny Mabel's story!" So thank you, Max Lowe, for giving me the idea!

Thank you to Annabelle Fenwick, for reading early drafts, calming me down, and answering my many Mabel questions.

Thanks to Rachel Roberts and Martha Price, for reading through the recipes, and helping with directions on how to make lavender wands!

As always, thank you to my wonderful parents, for encouraging me to write the books of my heart.

And last but by no means least, thanks and love to Jon, Sebastian, Oliver, Ben, and Juliette, for putting up with me while I write!

TURN THE PAGE
FOR A SNEAK PEEK AT

Lucy Castor

Finds Her Sparkle

By NATASHA LOWE

LUCY CASTOR DID NOT LIKE CHANGE. IT MADE her queasy and uncomfortable, and she tried to avoid it at all costs. Luckily, she had lived her whole life in the little western Massachusetts town of Hawthorne, in the same clapboard house on the same street with the same set of parents, so change was not something Lucy had to deal with very often. And when it did come along, she could usually cope with it, like the time her mother decided to make chicken on Monday instead of spaghetti, or insisted Lucy wear a skirt and not her usual sweatpants when they went out for dinner. Or the time her parents replaced their old green sofa (the one Lucy felt certain could fly if she knew the right magic words) without asking her first. These things were mildly upsetting (well, the sofa was heartbreaking) but Lucy generally recovered quite quickly, and life would go on in its familiar, comfortable groove.

At least until the weekend before she entered fourth grade, when a series of monumental events shook Lucy's world, and everything began to change.

I T WAS DELICIOUS TO BE HOME, LUCY THOUGHT, standing in the middle of her bedroom. The Castors had been gone all summer, visiting Lucy's grandmother in Vermont, and although this had been absolutely wonderful, there was nothing more exciting than being back in your own house. Especially when you were about to see your best friend, Ella, for the first time in eight weeks.

Wanting to wear her purple shirt with BEST FRIENDS ARE MAGIC written across the front, Lucy skipped over to her closet. She knew it would be in there, because she hadn't taken it to Vermont. The shirt had been a gift from Ella, two years ago on Lucy's seventh birthday. It was definitely on the small side now, but it made Ella smile when Lucy wore it. And something magical always seemed to happen whenever she put it on.

Tugging at the handle of her old pine closet, Lucy could feel the wood had swollen in the humidity. With an extra-hard pull she yanked the door open and gave a gasp of shocked surprise. For an instant Lucy froze, staring inside before quickly slamming the cupboard shut.

Heart pounding, she raced across the hall to her parents' bedroom, where she found her father putting on socks amid a jumble of unpacked suitcases, and her mother still lying in bed. Both these things were highly unusual, because the family had been home for a whole day already, and Mrs. Castor usually unpacked straightaway, plus she always got up early on weekends. But Lucy didn't have time to worry about such matters now. There were far more important things to deal with.

"There's a gnome in my closet," she panted, grabbing her father's hand. "With a long white beard and a red jacket. And he didn't look too happy to see me. He was frowning."

"Probably hanging up your things," Mrs. Castor murmured from the bed.

"No, he wasn't. He was just standing there with his

arms folded. Come on, Dad, please hurry," Lucy said, tugging him back to her room. With a grand flourish she opened the closet door, but there was nothing in there except clothes. Lucy pushed aside the hangers, peering to the back of the cupboard.

"I can't believe it. He's gone. I should have asked him what he was doing. But I was too scared." Lucy gave a shiver.

"I wish I'd seen him," Mr. Castor remarked.

Lucy pointed to her fluffy red sweater hanging at the front of the cupboard. "That was the exact cherry color of his jacket, and he wore these strange gold shoes with toes that curled up at the ends." She closed her eyes, picturing the shoes in her head. "They were more like slippers than shoes, very narrow and sparkly."

"Sounds like a well dressed gnome."

"He was," Lucy said, and then with rising excitement added, "Hey, Dad, look at this." Crouching down Lucy leaned inside the cupboard and touched the floor. She held up her fingers, which had tiny gold sparkles stuck to them. "From his shoes," she whispered, breathing hard.

This was different from the glitter she had used to decorate last year's Christmas presents; the home-made Popsicle stick picture frames she had hidden at the back of her cupboard. That glitter wasn't nearly as sparkly. Lucy was sure of it. She was quite certain. These sparkles were more shimmery, more golden, and she swept some into her hands as evidence.

Scrambling to her feet, Lucy darted over to her bedside table. She carefully brushed the sparkles into the open drawer, grabbed her special notebook, and sat on the edge of the bed. "I'm going to draw a picture of him, Dad. To show Ella when she comes over." Just the thought of Ella coming over made Lucy start to bounce with happiness. She was aching to see her best friend again. "Joined at the hip," that's what Lucy's dad always said, while Lucy's mom liked to call them "two peas in a pod." They had met on the first day of kindergarten and been inseparable ever since.

"She's going to be so mad she missed seeing him," Lucy said, looking up at her dad, eyes shining. "But she's going to be so excited when I tell her."

Lucy and Ella spent all their free time searching for signs of magic together. They had uncovered tiny (possibly fairy) footprints in the woods near Lucy's house, a bluish speckled stone that had to be a fossilized dragon's egg, and an old key in the garden, which the girls knew unlocked a secret door. They just hadn't managed to find the door yet.

"That's what we're going to do today," Lucy said, drawing a pair of curly-toed shoes on the page. "Go on a gnome hunt. We were going to make magic potions, but this is far more important. We'll search the attic and the basement and then camp out in my cupboard. He's bound to come back."

"I hope so," Mr. Castor said. "But maybe gnomes are scared of humans, Lucy? You could have frightened him away."

"He'll be back," Lucy said with confidence, sketching in the gnome's red jacket.

After eating a bowl of cold cereal Lucy went outside to wait for Ella, taking her notebook and mini binoculars with her. The mini binoculars were perfect for searching out signs of magic as well as spying on the robin's nest in Mrs. Minor's tree next door.

Lucy wanted to locate the magic wands that she and Ella had hidden beneath the rhododendron bush at the end of the yard. Putting her hand under the bush, she felt around and pulled out two sticks decorated with glitter and bits of moss. Each one had a purple ribbon tied around the handle end. Lucy waved her stick (the one with the most glitter) in the air and whispered, "Sparkalicious," which was the magic word she and Ella had invented.

Closing her eyes, Lucy sat very still, the grass soft and warm beneath her. She was sure she could feel magic close by. Probably seeing the gnome this morning had something to do with it, Lucy decided. A bee buzzed softly, and the air smelled faintly of lavender. Lucy breathed deeply and gave a contented smile. This was a perfect "petunia moment."

It had been Lucy's dad who first came up with the idea of petunia moments. Mr. Castor's father, Lucy's grandfather, had been a stickler for time, checking his watch regularly and tapping the glass face when he wanted to hurry everyone up. Lucy's dad said he was so busy worrying about time that he never had any left over to "smell the petunias," which meant noticing all the small, wonderful things that happened in a day, the sort of things you would hurry right by if you weren't paying attention.

A petunia moment could happen anytime, when you suddenly realized that the moment was about as perfect as it could get. Being handed a scoop of your favorite ice cream, for example, or when Lucy was snuggled on the sofa between her parents, listening to her dad read *The Hobbit*. But the petunia moments that Lucy loved the best were the enchanted ones like this, when you knew, with every cell in your body, that magic was definitely nearby. In fact Lucy had a strong suspicion that she herself might actually have magical powers. She was waving her wand in circles when the back door banged open and Ella called out, "Hiya!"

With a loud squeal Lucy scrambled to her feet. "Ella, you're not going to believe this, but I saw a gnome this morning! A real one," Lucy yelled, spinning around. "Ella?" she said again, staring at the girl with the swishy blond ponytail, the short jean shorts, and a cropped white T-shirt with the words SPARKLE GIRL spelled out in pink glitter.

It was definitely Ella, because her face looked the same, and she had on her little gold hoop earrings. But this was not the Ella Lucy knew. That Ella wore crumpled T-shirts and baggy gym shorts, just like Lucy had on now. She wore her hair loose and unbrushed, and she never tilted her head to one side or gave a cute little wave or said "hiya," like this Ella was doing. And never, in a million years, would she have worn a cropped white T-shirt with SPARKLE GIRL printed across the front.

The sparkle girls were part of a hip-hop dance troupe that took lessons at the Sunshine Studio in town. Some of the kids in their class were in it, and last year at recess Molly, Summer, and May used to practice routines, dancing about in their sparkle shirts with their ponytails swishing, while Lucy and Ella mixed up magic potions on the grass, laughing at how the sparkle girls didn't like to get dirty.

Glancing down, Lucy noticed that her legs were streaked with earth, and her BEST FRIENDS T-shirt had a hole under the arm and a faded chocolate stain on the front. She picked bits of grass out of her long brown hair, which she knew was a tangled mess. Normally, none of these things would have bothered Lucy one bit, but standing next to this new glittery Ella made her suddenly self-conscious and shy. Ella's face looked all dewy and fresh, and Lucy couldn't help feeling like a sweaty little mouse with her huge brown eyes and slightly crooked front teeth. Neither of the girls spoke right away, and Lucy rubbed at her shirt with a finger.

"Gosh, I can't believe you can still fit into that," Ella finally said, giving her ponytail a shake. The girls had always been pretty much the same height, but Ella seemed to have grown at least two inches since they last saw each other. Or maybe it was just her high, bouncy ponytail, making her appear taller. She glanced at Lucy's magic wand and then looked away, as if she didn't know what it was. An ache lodged in Lucy's chest, and she dropped her wand on the grass. "So how was your summer?" Ella asked with a bright, sparkly smile.

"Good." Lucy nodded, thinking of all the things she had been storing up to tell Ella and how silly they now sounded in her head. Finding a new bird's nest for her collection, trying to come up with a flying spell at her grandmother's house, but most important of all, discovering the gnome in her closet. "When did you become a sparkle girl?" Lucy blurted out, unable to stop herself.

"May wanted me to join the dance troupe. I didn't have much else going on this summer, so"—Ella gave a shrug—"I went along to watch one day, and it's actually really fun." With another swish of her ponytail Ella gave a quick demonstration, performing some fancy hip-hop moves. "You should join too, Lucy. Honestly, I think you'd love it. I never thought I would, but I do."

"I'm not very good at dancing," Lucy said, wondering if Ella was teasing her and this was all a big joke. "I'd hate everyone looking at me."

"There's a show coming up at the end of September," Ella continued, hip-hopping around the yard. "You have to come and watch us. You just have to."

Clearly Ella was not joking, and Lucy swallowed the lump in her throat. She felt as if she had missed an important summer assignment—how to prepare for fourth grade. Obviously, the list included: 1. Become a sparkle girl. 2. Start wearing your hair in a high, bouncy ponytail. 3. Branch out and make lots of new friends who have nothing in common with your old best friend. And number 4, the most upsetting of all—give up caring about magic. Ella hadn't asked one single question about Lucy's gnome since she'd mentioned him, and Lucy could feel her lip trembling.

"Are you all right, Lucy?" Ella asked in concern.

"Just a bit shaken up, that's all," Lucy said, wishing the conversation didn't sound so forced. But she had to tell Ella. It was too important not to, and lowering her voice, Lucy whispered, "I saw a gnome in my closet this morning. At least I think it was a gnome. It could have been an elf or a dwarf." There was a rather long silence, and Lucy added, "I thought we could try and find him." She didn't mention the picture she had drawn.

Ella looked embarrassed. "Come on, Lucy. You don't believe all that stuff anymore."

The ache in Lucy's chest grew sharper. She fiddled with her watch strap and dug her nails into her skin, trying to stop herself from crying. "I found a spectacular nest at my gran's house," she said. "If you want to see it."

"Cool." Ella glanced around as if waiting for someone else to show up. She started another little series of dance steps, not seeming very interested in Lucy's bird's nest either. "I'm practicing with May and Summer after lunch. You can come too if you want," Ella added. "I'm sure they wouldn't mind."

Lucy's throat grew tight. She had thought Ella was

spending the whole day with her, and for a moment she couldn't speak, worried her voice might start to wobble. She wanted so badly to talk with Ella, the old Ella, the one who would have raced upstairs to Lucy's room, wanting to see the sparkles she had found. It felt as if aliens had taken away her best friend and left a strange Ella look-alike in her place.

"Are you all right?" Ella asked, staring at Lucy in concern.

"I've just got a lot to do before school. You know, buy folders and pencils and stuff." Lucy could feel the tips of her ears starting to throb and grow warm the way they always did whenever she was upset, and she gave her hair a shake to cover them.

"I got all my things last week," Ella said. There was a rather long silence between the girls, and Lucy could feel herself getting a headache.

The morning dragged on as Lucy listened to Ella talking about May's swimming pool and how she had been invited to a big Labor Day party there and how Summer had taught her to do backflips off the deep end. Lucy hated to admit it, but she actually felt relieved when Ella finally left. And then she felt sad about being relieved, and even sadder that they hadn't gone up to her room and examined her newest nest together, the one she had found in the woods near her grandmother's house, the one with a crackly piece of snakeskin woven in among the twigs. Her grandmother had told Lucy that some kinds of birds put snakeskin in their nests to scare away flying squirrels, and Lucy had been so excited by this fact she couldn't wait to share it with Ella. But clearly the new "sparkle" Ella wasn't interested in Lucy's nest collection anymore. And she certainly wasn't interested in casting spells or making potions or wanting to search for gnomes.

In fact Lucy wasn't sure if she had anything left in common with her old best friend at all.